THEY'RE A WEIRD MOB

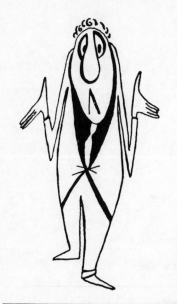

they're a weird mob

a weird

mob

A NOVEL BY NINO CULOTTA

ILLUSTRATED BY 'WEP'

HUMORBOOKS

First International
Humorbook Film Edition, 1966
Published by Ure Smith
and distributed by LS & P
188 Brompton Road, London, SW3
Printed in Hong Kong by
The Continental Printing Co. Ltd.

Originally published in Australia
by Ure Smith, Sydney and in the United Kingdom
by Nicholas Kaye
Copyright 1957 by Nino Culotta

This is a work of fiction, and is dedicated to all Australians who work with their hands, in gratitude for their very real contributions to my education.

Anyone who thinks he recognises himself in these pages, probably does.

N.C.

Chapter One

Wᴴᴼ the hell's Nino Culotta? That's what you asked yourself when you first picked up this book, wasn't it? Well I'm Nino Culotta. My father had me baptised Giovanni—John—well Giovannino is like Johnny, and Nino is an easier way of saying it. Or a lazier way, if you like. The Culotta family is not famous for doing anything the hard way. It is not famous for doing anything. Because as far as I know it doesn't exist. Not in my family, anyway. My family name is something quite different, but I can't use it here. Because this little book is about Australians, and if they knew who wrote it, some of them might put bricks through my windows. My windows cost me a lot of money and perspiration. To have windows you must first have a house, and I built my house with my own two hands and used the sweat of my head. Whenever I had a fiver I bought something, and whenever I had a week-end I built something. Sometimes concrete, sometimes brick, sometimes wood. And all costing plenty. And you know where I am now? I'm sitting outside my house early on Sunday morning, and the sun is just coming through the trees, and a dog is looking at me. In those trees there are kookaburras, and they laugh. Flying amongst those trees there are dollar birds, and they squawk. There are other birds whose names I do not know, but they all talk and the dew is shining on my grass, and I'm glad I built my house here. There are ants and flies and mosquitoes too, but everybody has to live, and I don't mind if these little ones live off me a bit. It would be nice if I didn't have to go to work to-morrow, but ants and flies and mosquitoes are not a satisfactory diet for a man as big as I am. My wife doesn't like them either. She's still in bed. I like to go to bed early and get up early, and she likes to go to bed late and get up late, so we don't see each other very much to talk. Except when there's a party, and nobody goes to bed. But she's a nice wife. She's an Australian. Not a black one. The ordinary kind, with one Irish ancestor and one French ancestor and some other kinds further back. I met her in a café, when she was trying to eat spaghetti with a spoon. This is not possible, I told her so, and she told me to mind my own business. You wouldn't think that could lead to marriage, but it can. So you see she is Mrs-what-my-real-name-is, and I don't want the bricks that might break my windows to fall on her head. So I call myself Culotta. But the Nino is true. I was baptised Giovanni.

My father had me baptised Giovanni because that was his own name and he was very proud of it. I do not know if he consulted my mother. But he often told me when I was a boy that I must grow up strong and brave because my name was Giovanni. I grew up strong enough, but bravery is a thing I haven't got. I had to have a good education too, because all Giovannis were knowledgeable men. We were big frogs in a small puddle in Piedmont, and when I left the village school and was taken to board with a relative whilst acquiring 'higher education', I found myself a small frog in the big puddle of Milano. It was in Milano that I first began to be interested in people as something other than just somebody else. I wanted to find out the reasons why they did the things they did. This curiosity got me much trouble. It also got me much hard work. Many foreigners came to

Milano, and I couldn't find out much about them, because I couldn't understand them. So I studied languages very diligently. When I thought I could speak English well enough, I began to ask questions of English people, and I got more trouble than when I was asking questions of the Milanese. But I also got a job with a big publishing house, interviewing foreigners and writing stories about them in the magazines. The French people were troublesome, because they said so much in answer to a question that much had to be left out of my articles; and the English people were troublesome because they said so little that I had to fill up from my imagination. What I imagined was not always true, and some of the English people could read Italian, and my troubles were plentiful.

One day my boss said to me, 'Nino, you are a pain in the head.' I agreed with him, because I could understand that he had troubles too. Then he said, 'We are going to send you to Australia.' Naturally I asked why, and he said, 'There are many Italians in Australia, and our readers would like to know how they are getting on. Also there are many Italians who want to go to Australia, and they would like to know more about it, but particularly more about Australians. I understand,' he said, 'that Australians speak English. You speak English, so you will go and ask questions, and write about what kind of people these Australians are.' I said, 'Yes, sir. Thank you very much.' And he said, 'Don't thank me, because I think it very likely that you will get knocked on the head and perhaps that will be a good thing.'

I went home to our village, and told my father that I was going to Australia, and he was very pleased. He said he always knew that one named Giovanni would show himself to be brave in the end. My mother said she would like to come too, and she and my father had an argument about

9

it, which my father won. I didn't feel brave. I felt curious. Because I had never met any Australians, although I heard that there were two in Firenze. That is Florence in English. My father said it would not be a good idea to go over there to meet them because (a) they might not be there now, and (b) I might get into more trouble and so miss the ship to Australia, and that would make my boss very irritable. So I said goodbye to all my relatives, and everyone else I knew. Some cried, and some looked pleased. There are many kinds of people in the world.

But at that time I thought the worst kind were what we called Meridionali. These are Italians from the south of Italy. They are small dark people with black hair and what we considered to be bad habits. We are big fair people with blue eyes and good habits. Perhaps it is a matter of opinion, and an Australian would lump us all together and call us 'bloody dagoes', but we didn't like Meridionali, and they didn't like us. Up in my country there were a few of them, and mostly they found themselves being officious in the police force. Perhaps subconsciously that is why we did not like them. Nobody likes police forces. Anyway, after I had said goodbye, I set off by train for Genova to catch my ship, but on the way I began to think that perhaps I would first have a look at the country where these Meridionali came from, as I had never been there. I had heard that Napoli was a good place to see them, and as the ship would be calling there and I could get there first by train, that is where I went.

I should mention here that another reason why I call myself Culotta is because there are many Meridionali in Australia. But there are lots more in Napoli. I was most conspicuous then, and got much trouble, so that I nearly missed my ship. An Englishman told me that if I hadn't drunk a lot of vino, and kept on yelling out 'dirty Meridionali' and other things, I would have been taken for an Englishman, and everything would have been all right. I blame most of it on the vino. Neapolitan vino is terrible to those who are accustomed to the vino of Piedmont. The English have said 'See Naples and die'. I saw Naples, and if I had drunk another bottle of vino, most certainly I would have died. However, I threw that last bottle at a mob of them who followed me down to the ship and I was pleased to see that it broke and splattered them with the horrible stuff. An ignorant steward on board told many people that I was chased down to the ship, and only just got on board in time to save my skin. This is not true. I told him so, and hit him on the top of the head with my fist. He fell down, but a lot of his steward friends attacked me and there was quite a battle in the alleyway, and I had to go and see the captain. He was a Venetian, and quite a nice man. He explained to me that all the stewards were Neapolitans and that practically all the passengers were Meridionali of some sort, who were emigrating to Australia, and that perhaps it would be as well if I remained in my cabin for the voyage. I explained to him that whilst no one could call me brave, it would be impossible for anyone to be frightened by a couple of hundred Meridionali, and therefore I was not worried. He said neither was he, in that respect, but I would have to keep to my cabin, all the same. I would be allowed out for meals, and to go to the toilet, and from four until five p.m. for exercise with one of his officers. When I said that this was poor treatment for a paying passenger, he pointed out that he was aware that I had not paid my own fare, and that he knew my boss very well.

So I spent the time on the voyage writing articles and

stories about Meridionali, which were posted in Fremantle, and which I learned later proved very popular with our northern readers. They were not published in magazines which had a sale in the south. I was very tempted to leave the ship at Fremantle, and travel overland at my own expense, but I didn't. My passage was paid to Sydney, and for some reason Sydney was where I wanted to conduct my investigations. I had been told, and had checked my informer's information with a map, that Sydney was to Australia what a flea is to an elephant.

Nevertheless, as Rome, to foreigners, is Italy, Sydney to me was Australia. And except for a few trips to nearby country centres, I have been in Sydney ever since. Five years ago I came ashore here, and I do not think I will ever leave it. My boss, after I had been here a few months, wanted me to visit other states, but I was so interested where I was, that I refused. Which is how I came to get the sack, in the long run, although I stalled him for two years.

During that two years I wrote many articles about Australia and Australians, basing my human interest stories on people I met in Sydney, and my geographical and economic articles on what they told me. I know now that much of it was wrong, but nobody in Italy worried about that, so I don't worry about it now. There was, however, much that I heard which could not be sent to my boss, because it would not make sense to him or to his readers. Suppose you were writing about one of your friends, and what you wrote had to be translated into a foreign language, you could describe his physical peculiarities, his dress, where he lived, where he worked, what he ate. But unless he spoke correct grammatical English, you could not translate what he said. Some colloquialisms perhaps you could manage, but in general, the conversations people have with each other cannot be reproduced in another language. I know our own Piedmont dialect, which is easier for the French to understand than for someone who has studied Italian, cannot adequately be rendered in English. And as for the Meridionali and the Sicilians, not even the Italian language can adequately reproduce their conversations. Although the Australian, and by that I mean the Sydney Australian, does not speak as badly as those who speak some of our Italian dialects, nor, as we say 'come mitraglio'—like a machine gun—he has a language which I badly wanted to reproduce for my boss. I tried, but it was impossible. Now that I have got the hang of it, I want to write about it, and since it cannot be translated into any other language, including English, all I can do is to put it down as I have heard it. To do this, I must put down also something about the people who speak it, and the situations where I heard it spoken. The troubles I had with it, too, must be described, so that Australians who read this book may realise how difficult it is for the foreigner, who has learned good English from books, to understand what the blazes they are yapping about!

Most Australians speak English like I speak Hindustani, which I don't. In general, they use English words, but in a way that makes no sense to anyone else. And they don't use our European vowel sounds, so that even if they do construct a normal sentence, it doesn't sound like one. This made it necessary for me, until I became accustomed to it, to translate everything that was said to me twice, first into English and then into Italian. So my replies were always slow, and those long pauses prompted many belligerent remarks, such as 'Well don't stand there like a dill; d'yer wanta beer or dontcha?' Now that I have had five years of practice, I find that I am able to think in English, and often in the

Australian kind of English, so that when some character picks me for a dill, he is likely to be told quick smart to suck his scone in!

Anyway, we dropped a lot of our Meridionali cargo in Fremantle, and more in Melbourne, and the captain allowed me to come out on deck between there and Sydney, after I had promised not to speak to anyone. So I saw Sydney for the first time the very best way—from the deck of a ship. And at the very best time—early in the morning, with the sun behind us. It was October, and the sun was beautiful. The Customs people were not, but the rest of our Meridionali had to be got ashore, and no doubt that accounted for them being irritable. My promise to the captain was no longer binding, so I said a few words. Which led to a nice little battle, which was ended by some Australian policemen. A big one, with silver stripes on his arm pointed to me. 'You,' he said, 'come here.'

I hit one more of the Meridionali, and walked over to him.

'You called me, sir?' I said.

'Where are your bags?'

'Over there, sir.'

'Get 'em.'

Two other policemen joined him, so I thought I'd better humour him. I got my bags and came back.

'Come on,' he said.

I followed them out, and they went to a taxi, and the big policeman opened the boot and put my bags inside. One of the others opened the door of the taxi, and stood by.

'Excuse me, sir,' I said, 'where do we go?'

He said, 'Get in.'

I got in, and the one by the door shut it, and the big one said to the driver, 'Get going.' The driver started up and

14

went up the street a little way, and then said, 'Where to, mate?'

I said, in a very dignified manner, 'It appears to me, sir, that since you are acting under the orders of the constabulary, you are undoubtedly well aware of our destination.'

He said, 'Cut the bull. An' don' call me sir. Where yer wanner go?'

Some of this I understood, and it was surprising. 'Do you not know?' I said.

'No,' he said.

'No?'

'No.'

'Oh.'

After a while, he said, 'Well we can't sit 'ere all bloody day; where we goin'?'

I was silently translating what he said into what I thought he meant in an English I understood, and translating this into Italian, and working out my answer in Italian, to be translated into English, all of which was taking some time, when he suddenly seemed to become very irritable and said, 'Gawd I've been drivin' this bloody thing since one o'bloody clock this mornin' an' now it's bloody near time for lunch an' I 'ave ter get landed with a bloody ning nong who doesn't know where he's bloody goin'. Will the Cross do yer?'

By the time I had worked out a few words of this speech, we had arrived somewhere, and he was getting my bags out of the boot. I got out also, and said, 'Excuse me, sir, but do you mind telling me where I now am?'

'Kings Cross. Three bob.'

'Excuse me, sir, but do you mind telling me where I now am?'

He shouted very loudly, 'KINGS BLOODY CROSS!'

I said this to myself two or three times, and decided that it must be the name of a suburb. So I said, 'Why?'

'Why what?'

'Why am I in Kings Bloody Cross?'

'Because I bloody brought yer . . . three bob.'

'I do not understand what you say, and I do not understand why I am where I am, but I thank you. Could you please inform me, please, where is some place where I may be able to obtain some food?'

'Anywhere around here,' he said. 'Are yer gunna pay me the three bob or ain't yer?'

'I beg your pardon?'

'Look mate, I brought yer from the bloody dock, an' you owe me three bob. Do I get ut or don't I?'

I caught the word 'Owe' and said, 'I am reminded of something. You have transported me to this place, and I would like you to inform me how much is my fare, please?'

He became very irate again, and said in a loud voice, 'Strike me bloody 'andsome, I just told yer. Three bob.'

'How much is the fare, please?'

He said, 'Oh-h-h!' and something I didn't understand, then pushed his cap back, and scratched his head. Then he said, very slowly and distinctly, 'Look mate, have–you–any–money?'

This was very good English, and I answered immediately, 'Yes.'

'Have–you–three–shillings?'

Again I was able to answer immediately, and I was wishing he would always speak as clearly as this. I said, 'Of course, I have three shillings.'

Then he seemed to acquire a great rage, and said, 'Well bloody give ut to me before I call the bloody cops or do me block or some bloody thing. Give us me three bob.'

He was holding out his hand, so I assumed he wanted three shillings. I gave him three shillings. He said, 'Any man takes this game on's not right in the nut.' He got into his taxi and drove away without even saying thank you.

I am able to understand now how troublesome I must have been for him. But at that time I understood only 'Have you any money' and 'Have you three shillings.' It was only after much experience with the language, and with taxi drivers, that I was able to work out what must have been the other things he said. At the time, I thought he was of a type qualified to live in Reggio Calabria, and was very sorry I had given him three shillings, instead of a bump on the head. But he was gone, and there was I, standing on the footpath of a place I thought was called Kings Bloody Cross, wondering where I was going to sleep, that night, but more urgent and important, where and what I was going to eat that day.

B

Chapter Two

To myself I said, 'This is what I will do, I will get myself a room in a hotel, then I will eat, and then I will buy a newspaper. In this newspaper I will see some work advertised, and I will do some work, and thereby meet some Australians. Working Australians. Because I am sure these are the kind of Australians my boss will want me to know about.'

Opposite to where the taxi had left me, there was a hotel called the 'Mayfair'. That is where I went. I obtained a room and a key, and deposited my two bags. When I discovered the prices charged, I knew I would not be able to stay there for very long, but the food was quite good, and I had a nice lunch. Then I went out. A boy was selling newspapers on a corner, and to him I said, 'Have you a newspaper in which work is advertised?'

He said, ' *'Erald's* the rag,' folded a paper, and put it under my arm. I felt in my pocket, and took out a large coin, and gave it to him. He said, 'Bit sunburned sport!'

I said, 'I beg your pardon?'

He said, holding out the coin, 'Right size, wrong colour.'

'Oh,' I said. 'I am very sorry.' I found a two shilling piece and gave it to him. He gave me change and said, 'Orright if ut comes orf, sport.'

'I beg your pardon?'

'Skip ut.'

He ignored me, and resumed calling out the names of his

papers. What he said was quite unintelligible to me, but apparently not so to other people, who were stopping and buying. I returned to my room to study my paper. There appeared to be much work advertised, but nearly all of it demanded abilities which I did not possess. However, one appeared possible. It read, 'Builder's labourer. Must be strong. Experience not necessary. CY 3301 after five.'

I went back to the newsboy, and showed it to him. I said, 'What mean these letters and figures? Are they a telephone number?'

He said, 'Ain't a cricket score, sport.'

'Is it a telephone number?'

'Yeah, wot else could ut be?'

'And this "after five". They mean what?'

'Means ring 'em after five o'clock.'

'To-night or to-morrow morning?'

'How would I know? You a builder's labourer?'

'No. But I could try to be.'

'Yer not right in the scone.'

'I beg your pardon?'

'Look sport, get lost will yer? I can't stand 'ere maggin' ter you all day. Got me work ter do.'

It was three o'clock, and I said to myself, 'Talking to this boy is unprofitable, because I do not understand what he says. Until five o'clock, therefore, I will walk, and observe this Kings Bloody Cross, and perhaps find somebody who speaks English. There are many questions I wish to ask.' So I walked around, and looked at the shops, and listened to people talking. Some were speaking Italian, but this did not interest me. Some were speaking German, and some French. Many were speaking Australian, most of which I could not understand. Outside a place called 'The

Arabian' from which came a strong smell of coffee, two well dressed men were speaking English.

I said, 'Excuse me gentlemen. You are speaking English. It is nice. I also speak English.'

One of them said, 'Congratulations.'

I said, 'Have I your permission to converse with you in English?'

The other one said, 'No.'

'May I then be permitted to buy you some coffee?'

The first one said to his friend, 'Come on. This place gets worse every day.'

This friend said, 'It's the Cross, old boy. Types you know.'

They walked away. This, I thought, was very rude, and I called after them, 'You gentlemen are very rude types.'

A man in a tobacco kiosk alongside said, 'Yer won't get any change outer them, mate. They're radio actors. No work, no money, no manners. Two bob an' one suit, that's them.'

'One can never judge by appearances,' I said. 'They spoke very good English.'

'Yeah. If yer like that sort of English. Speak a bit like 'em yerself. You in radio?'

'Oh no. I hope to be a builder's labourer.'

He seemed to think this was extremely funny. There were tears in his eyes when he stopped laughing. I said, 'Why do you laugh?'

'You. Standin' there solemn an' sayin' that. That's the best I've heard fer a long time."

I did not understand, so I asked him, 'Have you any Italian cigarettes?'

'No Italian. Got English.'

I bought a packet, and he said, 'Builder's labourers always

20

smoke English cigarettes.' He was laughing again as I walked away.

I walked down a hill and came to a park. Across the park was the harbour. I walked to it. On the edge of a small landing two bare-footed urchins were arguing. A small dead fish lay between them. They had fishing lines in their hands, and their feet dangled over the water.

'I tell yer ut's a morwong.'

' 'Tisn't. Ut's a drummer.'

'Ut's a morwong.'

'Ut's a drummer.'

'My old man's caught 'undreds o' morwongs. Ut's a morwong.'

' 'Tisn't.'

' 'Tis.'

'Ay mister? Ain't that a morwong?'

'Any mister'd know ut's a drummer ain't thet right mister?'

I pointed to the fish and said, 'Do you wish to know what that is?'

The chorus said, 'Yeah.'

'It is a fish. A dead fish.'

Their faces immediately became without expression, and their eyes unwinking, looked at me for a long time.

Then one said, 'You ain't funny.'

'The man at the tobacco shop thought I was very funny.'

'Yer look funny . . . but y'aint funny see.'

'I am an Italian.'

'Y'aint.'

'I am an Italian.'

'Y'aint. We seen a lot o' Italians, ain't we?'

'Yeah. Italians are little blokes.'

'Yeah. Tony Pozzi's Italian. He's a little bloke.'

'Many Italians are big like me.'

'Pigs.'

'Yeah, pigs.'

'Big Italians are not pigs.'

'Big Italians are Greeks. Ain't they?'

'Yeah. Old man Sponos.'

'Yeah. Old man Sponos.'

'Please do not call me "old man Sponos".'

'Y'aint old man Sponos. Old man Sponos' got the fruit shop.'

'Yeah. We seen 'im 'undreds o' times.'

'I am an Italian.'

'Y'ain't. Yer can't tell a drummer from a morwong.'

'Italians are little blokes. An' they know about fish.'

'Yeah, Tony Pozzi knows about fish.'

'Tony Pozzi's got the fish shop. We seen 'im 'undreds o' times, ain't we?'

'Yeah. 'Undreds o' times.'

'You do not believe that I am Italian?'

'No . . . yer too big.'

'Yeah. An' yer don't talk like one.'

'Yeah, Tony Pozzi talks like one.'

'Yeah. Old Tony Pozzi. Don-a-touch-a-da fish! Don-a-touch-a-da chip. Get-a buggery out-a-da shop. I give you good-a belt.'

They shouted with laughter, wriggling their toes together, their bent backs showing that I was dismissed. I was an impostor. A fake. I walked sadly away, and back up the hill. In the doorway of a large building, which appeared to be a place where trams were repaired, a man in a dark blue uniform with a leather bag hanging at his side, was smoking a cigarette.

I stopped and said, 'Good afternoon, sir.'

He looked at me for a while, and said, 'Wodda yer want?'

'Excuse me, sir . . . but could you tell me what the name of that vehicle which is now approaching may be?'

'Wot vehicle?'

'That one approaching down the hill.'

'Wot, the tram?'

'Do you call it a tram?'

'Wot else would yer call ut?'

I was surprised. I said, 'That is exactly what we call it in my country.'

'Wot's your country?'

'Italy.'

'Yeah.' He looked disbelievingly. 'Yer don't look like an Itie ter me. More like a Jerry.'

'What please, is a Jerry?'

'A Hun. A German. Or somethin' that goes under a bed. Something.'

'I am not a German. I do not like Germans.'

'Neither do I. Can't stand 'em. Wot part of Italy yer come from?'

'Piedmont.'

'Wot part o' Piedmont?'

I told him.

'Wot's yer name?'

I told him.

'Yeah. Could be. Was yer old man the mayor?'

I began to get excited. 'My father is mayor of our village, yes.'

'Yeah. Yer look a bit like 'im.'

'It is not possible that you know my father?'

'Not personally. Knew 'im ter look at. Cranky old bastard.'

He seemed to be referring to me or to my father as a

23

bastard, but I was too curious to be insulted. 'You have been in my village?'

'Sort of. I was a prisoner o' war there. Just outside your dump.'

'Ah. A prisoner of war. Yes, you were captured by our soldiers in North Africa?'

He appeared to become quite irritable. 'Captured by your mob? Don't gimme the tom tits. You Ities couldn't capture a bloody grasshopper.'

I did not know what this meant, and was trying to puzzle it out, when he said, 'No, the Jerries got me, mate. Comin' outa Greece. Sunk the destroyer we was on. Is yer old man still kickin'?'

'I beg your pardon?'

'Yer old man. Yer padre. Is 'e morto yet?'

'Non è morto, mio padre. Parla Italiano, Lei?'

'No, don't speak yer lingo mate. Picked up a few words, that's all. Like "dove va" an' "baccai mi". Learnt 'em from a sheila.'

'What please is a sheila?'

'A sheila? A bint. A ragazza.'

'Ah yes. Soldiers soon find the ragazze.'

'Not bad sheilas in your country. I'll say that fer 'em. Gotta go now, 'ere's me tram. So long. Be seein' yer.'

He swung onto a tram, coming out of the shed, and left me thinking of the smallness of the world, and of the ways of soldiers with girls. We thought all our girls were locked up when the Australians were working outside their compound, but apparently some got out. I reminded myself to tell my father. As mayor of the village at the time, he would be most interested. Then I decided, perhaps no. I have sisters.

I walked on up the hill. I was thinking, 'Supposing I get

24

this job, I will have to tell my boss. He is paying me. It would not be honest to be paid by two people. I will tell him and he will decide what is right to be done. I will tell him how much I earn as a builder's labourer, and he will decide.'

I stopped outside a hotel called 'The Mansions'. The bar doors were partly open, and there were a lot of men drinking beer. I was a little thirsty from my walk, so I went in. A woman approached me, and said, 'Wot'll ut be?'

'If you please, I would like to drink some beer.'

She said, 'Schooner or middy?'

After a while, I said, 'If you please, I would like to drink some beer.'

She said much louder, 'Schooner or middy?'

There was a man alongside me who had no coat on. He said to me, 'How long have you been in Australia, mate?'

'I have arrived in Australia today.'

'That explains ut. Those big glasses are called schooners and those small ones are called middies.'

'Now I understand,' I said. 'Thank you.'

The woman said, 'Schooner or middy?'

'If you please, I will have a middy.'

The man with no coat said, 'Have one with me.'

I said, 'Thank you sir, I would be delighted.'

He said, 'Two middies, Jean.' Then to me, 'Where do you come from?'

'I am an Italian.'

'Are you? You don't look ut.'

'In Italy,' I said, 'there are two kinds of people. Those who live in the north, and those who live in the south. I am of the north.'

'Are they all big blokes like you?'

'What, please, is a bloke?'

'Eh? Oh, everybody's a bloke. You're a bloke. I'm a bloke. We're all blokes.'

'Oh, I see. Like what the Americans call guys?'

'Yeah, something.' He handed me the beer, and raised his own to his lips. 'Cheers.'

I replied, 'Cheers,' and drank some of my beer. It was very good.

He said, 'Tasted Australian beer before?'

'No. This is the first time.'

'Best beer in the world. Puts a gut on yer, though. Wodda yer do for a crust?'

'I am sorry. I do not understand the Australian patois. Could you please use English words?'

'Sure, you'll get used to our slang if yer live long enough. How do you earn your living?'

'I am a writer.'

'In Italian?'

'Yes. In Italian.'

'They tell me it's an easy language to learn?'

'It is not as difficult as English.'

'Yeah, English is a bastard of a language.'

'I think Australian is a bastard of a language.'

He laughed, 'You're learning already. Your turn.'

'What is my turn?'

'Your turn to shout.'

'Why should I shout?'

'Because I shouted you.'

'I did not hear you shout at me.'

He thought for a while and said, 'I get ut. When you buy a bloke a beer, it's called a shout, see?'

'Why is that?'

'Haven't a clue, but that's what it's called. I shouted for you, now it's your turn to shout for me.'

26

'I was only a little thirsty. I do not think I wish another drink.'

He looked quite stern. 'In this country, if you want to keep out of trouble, you always return a shout, see?'

'It is the custom?'

'Bloody oath it's the custom. Your turn.'

'Would it be all right if I bought a drink for you, and did not have one myself?'

'No it wouldn't be all right. That's the worst insult you can offer a man.'

'Why?'

'Means you don't think he's good enough to drink with.'

'Oh. Then I will shout.'

'You better.' He called to the woman, 'Jean . . . two more.'

She approached us, and said 'Something similar?'

I said, 'Yes. I wish to shout.'

She looked at me as though I had said something wrong, but got two more beers. I raised mine, and said, 'Cheers.'

My friend said, 'Cheers.'

I said, 'Wodda yer do fer a crust?'

'Me? I do shift work fer the—hey! Did you hear wot you said?'

'Yes, I said wodda yer do fer a crust.'

'You got a good memory.'

'Yes. I am a bloke.'

'Yer not a bad sorta bloke, either, fer an Itie.'

'What is an Itie?'

'An Italian. You.'

'You do not like Italians?'

'Aw, they're all right, I suppose.'

'Probably you have met only Meridionali.'

'Wot are they?'

'Italians of the south.'

27

'Could be. Well, gotta be going. Might see yer here again sometime.'

'Could be.'

He laughed, 'So long.'

'So long.'

He laughed again, 'Won't take you long ter catch on mate.' Then he was gone.

The bar was beginning to get very crowded and noisy. I saw it was almost five o'clock. So I crossed the street, and went up to my room. I thought I would telephone this CY 3301 about half-past five. It would not do to appear too anxious. So I sat on the bed, and drafted a story for my boss. About landing in Sydney, about customs people, and policemen, and taxi drivers. Then I went down to the reception desk. I had the number written down on a piece of paper, and I gave it to the young lady there, and said, 'Would it be possible, please, for you to obtain for me this telephone number?'

She said, 'There's a phone in your room, Mr. Culotta.'

'There is? I did not observe it.'

'You go back to your room, and just lift the receiver. Then I will get your number for you.'

I said, 'Thank you very much,' and went up again. There was indeed a telephone there. I lifted the receiver and the girl answered immediately. I said, 'This is Mr. Culotta. Would you please . . .'

She interrupted me, 'Yes, Mr. Culotta. I'll get your number now. Hold the line, please.'

I waited feeling somewhat nervous. Then she said, 'There you are.'

Another female said, 'Hullo.' I said, 'Hullo.' She said, 'Hullo.' I said, 'Hullo.' The desk girl's voice said, 'You're through go ahead please.' The other female voice said

'Hullo.' I thought these greetings had gone on long enough. I would change them. I said, 'Good evening.' She said, 'Who's speaking, please?'

'Mr. Culotta.'

Then there was a pause, and she said, 'Yes.'

'Yes.'

'Do you want to speak to Joe?'

'Is it Joe who advertises for a builder's labourer?'

'Oh. Yes. Just a minute, I'll get him.'

I heard her footsteps, and then her voice calling, 'Joe! It's fer you.'

Heavier footsteps approached, and a man's voice said, 'Who is ut?'

'Some ding bat after that job.'

'Ding bat.'

'He sounds a bit crackers ter me.'

'Oh.' Then a loud voice said, ' 'Ullo.'

I had decided that this 'Hullo' was the same as our 'Pronto'. So I said immediately. 'Am I speaking with Mr. Joe?'

'Joe Kennedy here. Who's that?'

'This is Mr. Culotta.'

'Who?'

'Culotta.'

'You ringin' about that job?'

'Yes, please.'

'New Australian, are yer?'

'I am Italian, Mr. Joe.'

'Don' make no difference ter me, mate. Long as yer can do the job.'

'I have not the experience, sir. But I am big and strong.'

'Yer'll wanter be, mate. Ut's hard yacker. Diggin' foundations. Where yer livin'?'

'I am at the Mayfair Hotel, Kings Bloody Cross.'

'Gawd, yer wanter get outa there, mate. Yer'll go broke stayin' there. 'Ow long yer been there?'

'I arrived from Italy to-day.'

'Only ter-day? Don't waste any time do yer? 'Ow y'orf fer togs?'

'I do not understand.'

'Workin' togs, clothes.'

'Oh, I am clothed. Yes, thank you.'

'Okay. I'll give y'a go. If yer no good yer don' get paid. Fair enough?'

'Do I understand I have the job?'

'I'll give yer a start, mate. Be 'ere about seven in the mornin'.'

'Where, please?'

'Eh? Oh. Punchbowl.'

'Punchbowl. That is the name of the place where you are?'

'Yeah. Punchbowl. Get a train from Town 'All'd be yer best bet. An' when yer gets ter the station, turn right. No. Yer wouldn't know how ter nut ut out. I'll meet yer. Be at the station about seven, an' I'll meet yer with the truck.'

'I am to be at this Punchbowl station at seven o'clock to-morrow morning?'

'That's right matey. Seven o'clock.'

'Very well. How will I recognise you?'

'Don' worry about that, mate. I'll find yer.'

'Thank you sir. I will try to be on time.'

'Okay. An' listen mate. None o' this sir an' mister stuff, my name's Joe. Wot's yours?'

'My first name?'

'Yeah. Yer first name.'

'Nino.'

'Orright, Nino. See yer in the mornin', mate.'

'See you in the morning, Joe.'

There was a click on the line, and I replaced my receiver. This was good. I had a job. All I had to do now was to find out where this Punchbowl was, and how to get to it, and how long it would take to get to it, so that I would not be late. I would have my dinner, and then find out these things.

Chapter Three

THE girl at the desk found out for me. I would have to get a bus to Town Hall station, and then a train. I would have to leave about six o'clock. I would not be able to get breakfast so early, but she told me there was a place around the corner called the 'Hasty Tasty' which would be open. It never closed she said. After I had my dinner I went to look at it, so that I would know where to find it in the morning. It was not very elegant—it had a juke box. But it seemed to serve all kinds of meat, with eggs and onions and tomatoes, and some kind of coffee. Even at half-past five in the morning, which was the time I arrived, there were people there. There was a number of men who appeared to be going to work, and there were some horrible people of both sexes, who appeared to be closing a very long evening of enjoyment with much alcohol. They were playing the juke box. They were not sober.

I told the girl who came to my table that I was hungry, and I wanted plenty to eat, and it did not matter what it was. She brought me hamburger steak with bacon and onions and eggs and tomatoes. Apparently at this place they had much trouble with people who eat and do not pay, because she insisted that I paid before I ate. This I did. The coffee was the way it smelled, but the food was all right.

At the Town Hall I memorised the names of all the stations to Punchbowl, and then watched them through the window of the train. When I got out at Punchbowl, I did not know which side of the line Joe would be, so I waited in the middle of the overhead bridge. It was not yet seven o'clock. Indeed it was twenty past seven, and I was getting irritable, when I heard a voice say, 'You Nino?' Saying 'Yes,' I turned, and saw quite a young man, very slim, who wore heavy unpolished boots, dirty khaki shorts, an old blue shirt, and a very dirty old felt hat. He was holding out his hand. I took it, and said, 'You are Mr. Joe?'

'Cut the mister, matey. 'Ow yer goin' mate orright?'

This last word I did not know. I said, 'I am delighted to know you.'

He said, 'Okay. Let's get crackin'. The truck's over 'ere.'

I followed him down the steps to a very battered old utility truck, in the back of which there appeared to be many tools for digging. We drove around two or three corners, and Joe showed me where he lived. He said, 'The job's up the hill,' and a little later, 'This is it.' 'This is it' was a block of land about fifteen metres wide and about fifty metres long, all covered with long grass which I learned later was called 'bloody paspalum', except for a cleared place where there were a lot of short flat boards on two sticks, with strings running between them. The boards on sticks looked like small benches for sitting. A thin, dark young man, wearing old boots, was sitting on one of them rolling a cigarette. He did not get up when we approached. He just said, in a very flat slow voice, 'Where yer been?'

Joe said, 'Had ter pick up yer new mate, mate. 'Ow yer goin' mate orright?'

'Yeah mate. 'Ow yer goin' orright?'

'Orright mate. Nino, this is Pat. Pat—Nino.'

Pat extended a hand, and said, 'Pleased ter meet yer.'

I shook hands with him and said, 'How do you do?'

33

He said, 'Orright mate.

Joe said, 'I gotta go an' see about that metal an' stuff, an' tee up the mixer. How long yer reckon, Pat? Coupla days?'

'You gunna help?'

'No matey, gotta finish up that other job.'

Pat said, 'Three days.'

'Orright. Ter-day's Friday. We'll pour on Wensdy. Okay?'

'Okay mate.'

'Come an' get the gear outa the truck. Where's yer togs, Nino?'

I said, 'Togs?'

'Yer workin' clothes? Like me an' Pat?'

'Oh. I do not have any.'

They both looked at me, so I said, 'I could take off my coat.'

Joe said, 'That might be an idea. Wodda yer reckon, Pat?'

'N-o-o . . . No can't 'ave 'im taking orf 'is tie. The neighbours'd think yer was a lot o' common workmen.'

'Could 'e take orf 'is hat?'

'Yeah. Yeah 'e could take orf 'is 'at. Look matey, I gotta go. See if there's some old togs in that bag o' Dennis's next door. I'll leave ut ter you. I'll try an' drop back this arvo an' see how yer goin'.'

'Yer better.'

'Why?'

'Don' we get paid this week?'

'Gees, that's right mate. Orright, I'll be back at lunchtime. D'yer bring yer lunch, Nino?'

'I am sorry, Joe, no. I did not know . . .'

'Orright. Give us a few bob an' I'll bring some sandwiches when I come back.'

'You want some money, Joe?'

34

'Yeah, give us a coupla bob.'

I held out some money, and he took three shillings. Pat said, 'Wot a bastard you turned out ter be.'

Joe said, 'Give 'im a go, mate. 'E 'asn't done any before, but 'e'll be orright. Give 'im a go.'

'Why didn't yer get me Mr. Menzies?'

' 'E was too busy, mate. See yer later.'

Joe went away in the truck, and Pat said, 'Come on.' We went next door. Pat said, 'The old chook here owns the block. We change in the laundry. She makes us a cuppa tea, we bring our own lunch.'

'I will remember. I will bring my lunch next time.'

'That's if yer still 'ere.'

'Yes, you think I might be no good?'

'Yer look a bit posh ter me for this game. Where der yer come from?'

'Italy.'

'Gees, a bloody dago. Last bloke we 'ad was a Jugo-Slav.'

'Was he any good?'

'No.' Pat dug into a canvas bag, and produced an old pair of khaki shorts, and a cement-covered and very torn shirt. He said, 'Get inter them. 'Aven't got any boots. Yer'll ruin yer shoes.'

'I will get some boots and bring them next time.'

'See 'ow yer go ter-day, first.'

He did not seem to have much confidence in me, so I determined I would work very hard. As I put the old clothes on, he said, ' 'Aven't 'ad much sun, 'ave yer?'

'No. I had to stay in my cabin during the trip.'

'Why?'

'It was the order of the captain.'

'Wot did yer do?'

'I stayed in my cabin.'

'Serves me right for askin'. Better take ut easy. This sun'll burn holes in yer. Wear yer shirt while yer workin'. Yer c'n take ut orf at lunchtime. Better wear this lid.'

He offered me a very battered and shapeless old straw hat. I put it on. I said, 'How do I look?'

'I don' give a bugger 'ow yer look. We better get started. One diggin' an' one shovellin'. Wot'll y'ave first, mattock or the shovel?'

I did not know these words, so I said, 'I will do whatever you say.'

Pat said, 'Coo, look at me. I'm a boss.'

We went back to the block, and he said, 'I'll start diggin'. You come be'ind me an' shovel ut out.'

He commenced digging between the strings, the butt of his cigarette hanging from his lower lip. He was burnt nearly black by the sun, and I stood behind him admiring the play of muscles on his lean back. He wielded the heavy mattock effortlessly, moving his feet forward only when necessary, and without breaking the rhythm of his steady strokes. The soil was light in colour, and appeared to me to be very hard. I let him get two or three metres ahead of me, then began shovelling it out as fast as I could. I soon caught up with him, and had to wait again. So we went along this row of strings, Pat swinging steadily, and I alternately shovelling furiously, and waiting. At the end of the row he stopped, straightened up and looked back. I was close behind him, waiting. He looked at the trench, at the soil I had thrown out and at me. He took out a box of matches and re-lit his cigarette. Then he stepped aside and pointed without words at his last digging. Knowing he was watching me, I worked very hard and fast, and was soon finished. I turned to him and he took out a battered old tobacco tin, and threw it to me.

'Roll yerself a smoke matey.'

'I am sorry. I am unable to make cigarettes.'

'Smoke tailor mades do yer?'

'I beg your pardon?'

'Tailor mades. Bought cigarettes. D'yer smoke them?'

'Yes I smoke them. Would you like one? I have some in my coat.'

'Not fer me, matey. Go an' get 'em an' have one yerself.'

'Thank you. It will be all right? If Joe comes back would he?'

'Bugger Joe. Have a smoke.'

I got my cigarettes, and returned. Pat was squatting on his heels. I sat on the ground. He appeared to be my boss for the day, so I would do as he did. He nodded his head towards the cottage behind us, and said, 'Bloke next door's a Chinaman.'

'A Chinese man?'

'Yeah. He don't like dirt in 'is backyard.'

'He does not?'

'No. So don't chuck ut so bloody far.'

'Chuck it?'

'Save yer strength. Yer don't wanter go chuckin' dirt all over the block. Pile ut up near the trench.'

'Near the trench. Here?'

'About there.'

'How deep must be this trench?'

'About a foot.'

'We do the trenches where all the strings are?'

'Yeah. Bloody clay.'

'Clay?'

'Yeah, she's a bastard when ut rains.'

'It is not raining.'

'Yer sure?'

'Of course . . . the sun is shining and . . . You make fun with me, I think.'

'Only kiddin' yer. How about havin' a go on the mattock?'

'You wish me to dig?'

'Yeah. I wish you ter dig.'

'Okay.'

'Anywhere yer like. Just foller the lines.'

'Okay I start here.'

I put the butt of my cigarette under my foot, and took the mattock. Very soon my shoes were filled with dirt, and I was perspiring heavily. It was hard work. My back began to get tired. I had to wipe the perspiration from my eyes frequently. But I did not like to stop. So I kept on digging, and I began to get very worried, because I did not think I could continue to do this all day. My arms were losing all feeling. Then I heard Pat say, 'Righto, matey. That's enough.'

I was very grateful, I straightened my back slowly, and said, 'Is enough?'

'Yeah. Come an' 'ave a cuppa tea.'

He had some tea things on a tin tray, and was sitting in the shade of the fence. I saw that he had done no work. This did not seem right. I said to him, very stonily, 'You have not been shovelling the soil.'

'Plenty of time, mate. Have a cuppa. Take milk an' sugar?'

'I will have some milk and sugar, please. But I think you should have shovelled the soil.'

'Aw, stop laughin', it'll keep. Here, get this inter yer.'

He handed me a cup of tea. It was hot, and sweet, and very very good. I was so thirsty.

'Have another.'

'Thank you, yes.'

I sat down and drank this one more slowly. 'Have a biscuit?'

'No, thank you.'

'Know wot I reckon?'

'What do you reckon?'

'I reckon you'll conk out about lunchtime.'

'Conk out?'

'Yeah, bust a gut. By lunchtime yer'll 'ave 'ad ut.'

'I see. I am not good?'

'Wouldn' say that, matey. Yer wanner take ut easy. No use goin' like a rat up a rope. Know how much I'd a done by now if I was you?'

'Much more?'

'Much bloody less. The shot's just keep pluggin' along. No sense in bustin' yerself.'

'I work too fast?'

'Yeah, take ut easy. Give us one o' yer tailor mades.'

I gave him a cigarette. I was feeling better now, and pleased with myself. He said I worked too fast. That was good. I said, 'The shovelling is easier than the mattocking.'

'Yeah, I'll get out that lot, an' then you can take the shovel till lunchtime.'

'It is all right, Pat. I can do the mattock.'

'I know!'

'I will go more slowly.'

'You take the shovel.'

'Very well.'

'Better get this tray back ter the old duck. Now take ut easy.'

I took up the mattock again, but worked more slowly. I thought maybe if I worked like this, I could go all day. I began to like the feel of the sun on my back, and there was not so much of the perspiration in my eyes. I would get

39

myself some boots, too. These shoes were no good. I would write about Pat and Joe when I got to know them better. I liked the way it was between them. Joe was the boss, but Pat was no servant. Could it be that in Australia there were no masters and servants as we knew them? Or was this case unusual? I would observe and find out. I would ask questions. This was an aspect of employer and employee relations which would be very interesting back home.

When I reached the end of the row, I paused for a moment to observe Pat. He used the shovel as he used the mattock, steadily and smoothly, with what seemed no effort. He did not throw the soil with the shovel, as I did. He let it turn in his hands, and the soil seemed to build itself into a row alongside the trench. He saw me watching him, and stopped. He said, 'Okay she's all yours.' He came over and took the mattock. 'Just stay behind me an' don' bust yerself.'

This I did, it was not too hard. Although when we got into the lumpy red soil that Pat said was called clay, it was harder. With an occasional pause for a smoke, he worked steadily, and I was able to keep up with him. Then the old truck appeared, and Joe stepped out. He carried a brown paper bag. He called out, 'Lunchtime, matey. Gunna work all day?'

Pat said, in his slow flat voice, 'I was gettin' so interested in me work I never noticed the time.'

'I'll bet yer was,' said Joe. 'How's ut goin'? Orright. How's the kid goin'?'

'He's goin' orright.'

'Good-o. Here's yer lunch Nino.' He threw the paper bag to me. I caught it.

'Thank you, Joe.'

'Think nothin' of ut, matey. Spondooliks, Pat.' He handed Pat an envelope. Pat put it in his hip pocket. 'Don' buy too many elephants. Give yer yours this arvo, Nino.'

Pat said, 'You comin' back this arvo?'

'Yeah. See yer about four.'

'Checkin' up on us, eh?'

'Der yez want a ride down in the truck, or don't yez?'

'Yeah, we do.'

'Well quit slingin' orf about checkin' up, or yez c'n bloody walk.'

'We'll be really pleased ter see yer. Yer such a nice man.'

'That's wot me girl says. Be seein' yer, matey.'

'See yer.'

Joe drove away, and we went to the laundry next door, and washed our hands. Pat went into the house, and came out with more tea. Then we sat in the shade to eat our lunch. Afterwards I took off my shirt, and lay down in the sun. I went to sleep. Pat woke me when it was time to start work again. I didn't want to start. I was sleepy and tired, and my hands were sore, but after half an hour I felt better, and we worked steadily all the afternoon, except for one bad moment when I thought I was going to faint. It was the sun which was very hot, and the constant stooping. Pat noticed me, and said, 'Yer gettin' too much sun on the back o' yer neck, matey. Go an' stick yer 'ead under the tap.'

I went into the laundry, and let the lovely cool water run all over my head and neck. It also ran all over my back and down my legs. When I came back, Pat said, 'Gees yer look like a drowned rat.' But I felt much better.

We were still digging and shovelling when Joe arrived to say, 'Knock off time matey.' He looked at the work and said, 'Gees yer'll finish that Mondy, Pat.'

Pat said, 'We might, but we're not pourin' concrete 'til Wensdy.'

'Why ain't we?'

' 'Cause we gotta tie the bloody steel, that's why.'

'Won't take all day tyin' steel.'

'If we finish this Mondy, ut will.'

'Yeah. S'pose ut will. Wilson's bringin' the metal on Mondy with the sand. I'll get 'im to bring the cement at arf past seven Wensdy. The mixer'll be 'ere then.' He walked over to me. 'Here's a couple and a 'alf fiddley dids, matey. Yer goin' orright. Put y'on first class award next week.' He gave me two pound notes and a ten shilling note.

I took them and said, 'I am all right, Joe?'

'Good as anybody y'd get, don't worry about that. Clean up an' I'll run yez down.'

We cleaned up in the laundry, and put the tools in the back of Joe's truck. We got in the front with him. Pat said, 'Yer goin' down the Bloodhouse?'

'Wouldn' drink there if yer paid me, mate. They got the worst beer in Sydney.'

'Yeah, ut's crook orright. Wot about the Belmore?'

'No matey. Too far. We'll go up ter the Bankstown. Wot about you Nino? Yer gunna pin one on?'

'What is this pin one on, Joe?'

'Knock one back. Gunna 'ave a drink?'

'I would like a drink yes.'

'Good-o. We'll go ter Bankstown.'

Pat said, 'Where's Dennis an' Jimmy?'

'They're up there already.'

'Well why didn' yer bloody say so?'

Joe did not reply, and we drove into this Bankstown. There was much traffic, and there were many people. Pat said, 'Where they at, the Cumberland or the Bankstown?'

'The Bankstown matey.' He turned right.

Then Pat said, 'Yer'll be at the North Bankstown in a minute. Where der yer think yer goin'?'

'Gotta find a place ter park matey.'

'Well let us out an' we'll wait fer yer.'

'Like hell I will.'

He parked the truck, and we walked back. I was ashamed of my very dirty shoes. Joe and Pat were now wearing clean trousers and shirts. I said, 'I am ashamed of my shoes.'

They both laughed. Joe said, 'Take 'em orf matey.'

Pat said, 'Yeah, chuck 'em ter the shouse.'

I paused to think about this, and Joe said, 'Come on, Nino, we was only kiddin' yer. Yer shoes are orright.'

'You are sure Joe? I do not wish to shame you in front of your friends.'

Pat said, 'Little gentlemen aren't we?'

'Not so little, either. Come on. There'll be worse foot-gear than yours in there.'

We went into the bar. It was very crowded and extremely noisy. Joe pushed his way through to the far end, where two young men yelled at him. One said, 'Gees the boss. 'Owyergoin' mate orright?'

'Orright mate. Wotta yez drinkin'?' The other one said, 'Champagne.'

Pat said, 'Well chuck us over a bottle.'

Joe said, 'Meet the new kid, Nino, this is Dennis. My brother Jimmy—Nino.'

They said together, 'Pleased ter meet yer.'

'He's an Itie,' said Joe.

'He's orright though,' said Pat. 'No slingin' orf.'

'My shout,' said Joe. 'I know what these bastards drink. Wot'll you 'ave Nino?'

43

I said carefully, 'I reckon I could knock over a schooner.'
They all laughed very much. I felt pleased. I also felt
proud that I was accepted into their company. I felt proud
of the two pounds ten shillings in my pocket, which I had
earned with my sweat. I was very tired, and very happy, and
very thirsty.

Chapter Four

Here I should describe my new friends, and the small organisation of which I was now a member. Whilst Pat was slim and dark, Dennis was broader and more muscular. He was not tall, but very well formed. His skin was smooth and brown, his hair dark brown and wavy, and his eyes were pale blue. They could become very cold when he was annoyed. Joe said he was a 'moody bastard'. Joe's brother Jimmy was totally unlike Joe, except that he was slim and wiry, as Joe was. He was very dark, with straight black hair and large dark eyes. His eyelashes were long, and curled upwards. He always listened to everything that was said, but seldom spoke himself. He had been in the army. Joe said he was a 'moody bastard' too. He and Joe were by trade, bricklayers. They were now a partnership, engaged in what is known as 'Spec. Building'. They bought a block of land, built a house on it, and then sold the house. Occasionally they built for a specific person, at a quoted cost, as in the case of the block on which Pat and I were working. Dennis was a brickie's labourer. Joe and Jimmy worked together on the brickwork, and Dennis 'kept 'em going'. Pat sometimes worked as a brickie's labourer, and sometimes as a general labourer, but he was paid as a brickie's labourer. I was the general labourer. Joe was the organiser, and there were always at least two jobs 'going'. Dennis and Pat lived with Dennis' parents, next door to Joe. Jimmy lived with Joe and his wife, Edie, but they told me he was 'gettin' married next Saturdy'.

When we left Bankstown hotel at six o'clock, we were not very sober. I had drunk five schooners of beer. I was not accustomed to manual labour in that hot sun. I was not accustomed to sandwiches for lunch. And I was not accustomed to drinking five schooners of beer. We were all a little hilarious. We stood in a group, in the street outside the hotel. Dennis and Pat knew a couple of 'fabulous drops' that they were going 'ter take ter the pictures'. In addition to being 'fabulous drops' these were also 'slashing lines', and 'One of 'em's old man owns a pub.' Jimmy's fiancée Betty was 'comin' up after tea'. Joe said, 'You look like bein' out in the cold, Nino. Yer don' wanner be out in the cold. Come on 'ome ter tea.'

I said, 'Joe, I do not think I could drink tea after all those schooners.'

'Well yer don't 'ave ter. Yer could go a feed, couldn' yer?'

This I did not understand. Dennis said, with a very affected English accent, 'What he means, old cock, is that your stomach requires nourishment. He invited you to share his humble repast: to visit his home and to be regaled with provender. Do you, or do you not, accept?'

This I did understand. But it was received with much merriment. And when I replied seriously, 'Thank you, Joe; I accept your kind invitation,' they put their arms around each others' shoulders, and were almost helpless with mirth.

'Gees, Nino,' said Pat. 'Yer'll kill me.'

'Nothin' ter wot 'e'll do to Edie,' said Joe. 'Come on let's get crackin'.'

We all fell into the truck, Pat and I in the back and the other three in the front. Jimmy drove. When we reached

46

Joe's place, Pat and I got over the tailboard, but the other three were still in the truck arguing. I heard Joe say, 'Ut's the carburettor, matey.'

Jimmy said, 'Manifold, more like.'

Dennis said, 'Ut's the whole bloody truck if y'ask me.'

'Nothin' wrong with the truck mate,' said Joe. 'She goes.'

'Only to the boneyard.'

'Wot's wrong with 'er? She does the work, don' she? She gets us there, don' she?'

'Only just.'

'Don' matter if it is only just, long as she gets us there.'

'One day she won't.'

'Orright one day she won't. One day you won't either. We all gotta wear out matey. When she wears out I'll get a new one.'

'She's worn out.'

'Pigs she is. There's a lot of life in 'er yet.'

Jimmy said, 'Ut's the manifold.'

Joe said, 'Carburettor more like.'

Pat interrupted, 'Yez gunna argue all night? Come on Den. We gotta meet those sheilas.'

Dennis got out. 'See yer ter-morrer, Joe. You be here ter-morrer, Jimmy?'

'Yeah, have a look at that manifold.'

'Carburettor, matey,' said Joe. 'We'll start on the carby.'

Jimmy didn't answer, and they got out. Pat and Dennis went into their place, saying 'See yer Mondy, Nino.'

I said, 'Goodbye Dennis. Goodbye Pat.'

Joe, Jimmy and I then went into Joe's place. Joe's living room was what I came to recognise later as typical for a suburban brick cottage. There was a central fireplace; a fawn patterned carpet, a sofa with two matching upholstered chairs, also fawn; heavy green curtains; a radio; and plenty

47

of ash trays. Joe indicated one of the chairs, 'Sit down, Nino. Take a load orf yer feet.' Then he raised his voice. 'Yer there, Edie?' A woman's voice answered from somewhere out the back. He said, 'Come 'ere. We got a visitor for tea.'

The voice shouted, 'Who is it?'

'You don' know 'im. Come 'ere an' meet 'im.'

She appeared. A slim woman of about Joe's age and colouring. I rose to my feet.

Joe said, 'Nino, this is my wife Edie. Edie, this is Nino. He's just started with us. He's an Italian. He's orright, though.'

Edie said, 'Pleased to meet you.'

I said, 'How do you do, Mrs. Joe.'

'Don' call 'er Mrs. Joe. Call 'er Edie. Wot's fer tea, Ede?'

'I got some fish. And there's some beans and potatoes.'

'Fair enough. How long will ut be?'

'It's cooked now.'

'Good on yer, Ede. Enough ter go round?'

'I always have enough on Fridays. I never know how many there'll be.'

'Just the four of us. 'Ave a drink with us before tea?'

'Wouldn't mind.'

She sat on the sofa and folded her hands in her lap. Jimmy sat beside her, and began rolling a cigarette. Joe went out, and I also sat down. There was silence.

Then Edie said, 'Is Betty coming over, Jimmy?'

'Yeah.'

'How is she?'

'Orright.'

There was another silence.

Edie said, 'How long have you been in Australia, Nino?'

'I arrived in Sydney yesterday.'

'Is that all? Do you like Australia?'

'I think I am going to like it. Yes.'

'I suppose it's a bit too soon to tell, yet.'

Not quite understanding this, I did not answer. Then Joe came in with two bottles. There was a very wide doorway between the living room and the dining room, and Joe placed the bottles on the dining room table, and opened them. He got four glasses from a cabinet, and began to fill them. When I saw it was beer, I said, 'Joe, I do not think I could drink any more beer.'

'Aw, course yer could.' He brought me a full glass. 'Get that inter yer. Ut'll do yer good.'

'Very well. I will try.'

He gave a full glass to Edie, and one to Jimmy, then taking the other he sat in the chair opposite me. He raised his glass and said, 'Cheers.' We all said, 'Cheers,' and drank some of the beer. Joe put his glass on the arm of the chair and took off his shoes. His feet were very dirty. He said to me, 'Get yer shoes orf, Nino. Give yer feet a rest.'

I said, 'My feet and socks are covered with soil, Joe. They are very dirty.'

'Don' worry about that. Get 'em orf.'

Edie said, 'We're used to dirty socks and feet in this house. Joe doesn't have his bath till after tea.'

'Take too long 'avin' a bath before tea,' said Joe. 'Sooner 'ave a beer.'

I said, 'Do you drink much beer, Joe?'

Edie said, 'Yes, he does.'

Joe said, 'No I don't. A few schooners after knock orf time, an' a couple o' glasses before tea. That's not drinkin' much beer.'

'Only about ten shillings a day,' said Edie. 'Only about three pounds a week.'

D

'Well wot's three quid a week? I got no other vices 'ave I?'

'I wouldn't know,' said Edie.

Jimmy looked at me and winked.

I said, 'Do all Australians drink beer?'

'No, not all mate,' Joe said. 'There's a few wowsers about.'

'What are wowsers?'

'Blokes that don' drink. Mind yer, I got nothin' against 'em. 'Ad a bloke workin' for me once, who didn't drink. Did 'is work orright. Good as anybody y'd get.'

Edie said, 'Do you drink much, Nino?'

'In Italy we do not drink beer.'

'Wodda yer drink?' said Joe. 'Plonk?'

'What is plonk?'

'Wine. All-round-the-world-fer-a-zac steam.'

'We drink wine, yes.'

'Beer's the only drink fer a workin' man. Whisky makes yer silly. An' plonk'll rot yer boots.'

He got up and emptied the other bottle into our glasses, despite my protests. We all said 'Cheers' again.

'Mind yer though,' he said, 'I won't stand fer a bloke drinkin' on the job. Never drink meself when I'm workin'. When yer knock orf. That's the time.'

Edie said, 'Are you married, Nino?'

'No, I am not married.'

'Never get married, mate,' said Joe. 'Yer life's not yer own when yer married.'

'You do all right,' said Edie.

'Jimmy's gettin' married next Saturday. Wants 'is 'ead read.'

'Leave Jimmy alone. Betty's a nice girl, isn't she Jimmy?'

' 'E'd have ter say she was, whether she was or not.'

'When do we eat?' said Jimmy.

Edie got up, 'Come on Joe, set the table.'

'You set ut love. I gotta talk ter me guest.'

'He's my guest, too.'

'No. No, love. I invited him. I gotta talk to 'im.'

'I'll talk to 'im,' said Jimmy.

'My brother,' said Joe in a disgusted voice. He went out with Edie.

I said, 'You wish to talk with me, Jimmy?'

'Not particularly.'

'There is no particular subject you wish to discuss?'

'No.'

He turned the radio on, and rolled himself another cigarette. We sat in silence. Then Joe came in.

'All set. Wanna wash yer 'ands, Nino?'

'Thank you, Joe.' I got up and followed him out the back door. He pointed to another door. 'In there mate.'

I went in. There was no place for washing hands. But the convenience that was there was very welcome. When I returned, Joe said, 'Bathroom's in 'ere.' I went into the bathroom, and washed my hands. Then we sat down to an enormous meal, which was washed down by numerous cups of tea. There was no conversation except what was necessary for eating, such as 'Pass the salt,' 'Pass the butter,' and 'Pass the sugar.' Only one phrase I did not understand. Joe said to Jimmy, 'Smack us in the eye with another hunk o' dodger, matey.' Jimmy gave him some bread, but I was unable to see the connection between the request and the reply.

After the meal I felt tired and sleepy. I requested permission to return to my hotel. Joe said, 'Know just 'ow yer feel, matey. First day of 'ard yacker knocks yer. I'll run yer down ter the station before I 'ave me bath.'

I was too tired to protest much. Jimmy said, 'So long,' and at the door Edie said, 'Come again Nino. It's nice to have a gentleman in the house for a change.'

51

Joe said, 'Wanna watch out, mate. She's takin' a shine ter yer.'

At the station, I thanked him for his hospitality, and he said, 'Think nothin' of ut. See yer Mondy matey. Arf past seven.'

I took a seat in the train, which was almost full. The people appeared to be wearing their best suits and dresses. I thought they were probably going to theatres and dances. I was sitting near the doorway of a carriage, with another seat opposite me. Sitting there was a man in a shabby grey suit. He was a lean man. He was staring at me rudely. I stared back, and soon saw that although his eyes were concentrated fiercely on me, his brain did not appear to be turning in his head. I decided he was drunk. I decided I would ignore him. Suddenly he leaned across the aisle, and shouted, 'Why don't yer go back to yer own bloody country? We don't want yer out here. This is our country. We don't want yer out here. Come out here takin' jobs an' think yer own the joint. Bloody dagoes. Why don't yer go back ter yer own bloody country?'

I looked over and saw a family of Meridionali. Two men who appeared to be brothers, a woman who could be their mother, one who could be the wife of one of them, and three small children. I thought they did not understand what was being said, but the tone of the man's voice would undoubtedly tell them that they were being insulted. They looked embarrassed, and pretended to ignore him.

'Don't understand me, eh? Don't know wot I'm talkin' about, do yer? Why don't yer? Why don't yer learn English? King's English. It's good enough fer me, ain't it?'

He sat back and fumbled in a trouser pocket, taking out a very battered cigarette. Then he leaned towards me, and said in a very normal conversational tone, 'Give us a light fer me pipe, mate.'

I lit his cigarette for him, which appeared to be what he wanted. He inhaled twice, then offered the cigarette to me. ' 'Ave a draw, mate.'

I shook my head.

'Trouble with this country there's too many dagoes in it. Takin' the bread an' butter outa the mouths of our wives an' children. Can't even speak English. Don' wanna speak English. Yabber, yabber, yabber. That's all they do. Yabber, yabber, yabber. This is our country. We fought fer this country, didn' we? Wot do we wanna let that mob in fer?'

The Meridionali were talking softly amongst themselves. He stood up abruptly and shouted fiercely at them. "Yabber, yabber, yabber. Wot are yer talkin' about? Nobody knows. Bloody spies the whole lot o' yer. White Australia! Bloody dago spies. Mussolini. Castor oil. Who won the war? We did, didn' we? Dagoes. Pinheads.' He sat down suddenly and again said normally, 'Give us a light fer me pipe, mate.'

Again I lit his cigarette.

'Take you, f'rinstance. You gunna let 'em take the bread an' butter outa the mouths of your wives an' kids? You gunna let them dagoes run this country? Yabber, yabber, yabber? You gunna let 'em talk that stuff out here? Dagoes an' Jerries an' Balts an' Poles an' Lithu-bloody-wanians? Wodda you gunna do about it? Wot's the Gov'ment gunna do about it? Give us a light fer me pipe, mate.'

I gave him my box of matches; after much fumbling he struck one. The cigarette was about one inch long. He held the match out six inches . . . he became cross-eyed. He puffed vigorously on the unlit cigarette and threw the match away. He handed me the box.

'Take you, f'rinstance. You're an Australian. You fought

fer this country. Do you yabber, yabber, all the time? Are you a bloody dago spy? Am I? When you get into a blue do yer pull knives? Knives all bloody over 'em. Pull knives. Australians don't pull knives. We fight with our fists, don't we? We don't pull knives, do we? Chuck 'em out. Chuck 'em out o' the country, chuck 'em out of the train.' He stood up again and yelled, 'Get outa the bloody train. It's not your train. This is our train. We bought our tickets didn't we? Whose taxes paid fer this train? I'll tell yer whose taxes. Our taxes, that's whose. Get out of our bloody train.' He stood swaying and glaring at them.

I said to them in clear slow Italian, 'Do not be alarmed. The man is drunk. He will not harm you. If necessary I myself will put him off the train.'

They smiled and nodded their heads, and gave me many expressions of thanks, and proceeded to talk animatedly amongst themselves, surprised and pleased to hear me speaking Italian to them. The moment I started to speak, the man turned quickly and stared hard at me. Then he sat down slowly, not taking his eyes from mine. For five minutes, unwinking, he stared at me in silence. I kept my face free of expression. Then he said, experimentally, 'Give us a light for me pipe, mate.'

I gave him the matches. He made no attempt to use them. He began muttering to himself, still staring at me, 'Bastards are everywhere. Man never knows who's wot. Knows wot I said. Looks like an Australian. Ain't. Never says a word. Starts talkin' yabber, yabber, yabber. Keep 'is bloody matches. Wouldn' use 'is bloody matches.' He leaned forward and tapped me on the knee. 'Parlez vous Français?'

I said, 'No.'

'Sprechen sie Deutsch?'

'No.'

'Speak English?'

'No.'

He breathed hard. He sat back. 'No,' he says, 'No. Don't speak anything he says. Talks yabber, yabber ter that mob. They yabber back at him. Bloody liar. Bloody spy. Knives all over 'em.'

I said, 'Please return my matches.'

He threw the matches to me.

I said, 'Thanks.'

We still stared at each other. He said, 'Now he talks English. Man never knows who's wot. Country ain't his own any more. Fought fer this country. Gotta fight ter keep it. Gotta fight. Who's left ter fight? Me. Whole damn country an' only me.' His expression became resolute. 'All right, it's up ter me. Fight 'em on me pat malone. Start with this mob. Chuck 'em orf the train.'

He stood up and moved towards the Meridionali. I called a warning. The man nearest jumped up. I saw a knife in his hand. I moved quickly and with my fist I bumped the Australian on the top of his head. He sat down, I picked him up, and put him back in his seat. The women were looking scared. I said to the other passengers, 'It is all right. He is not hurt. He is unconscious. He will recover soon.' No one answered me. I heard one woman say to her escort, 'Disgusting. Drunks and foreigners. What's the guard doing?' I did not hear his reply. I sat down. Then I remembered the knife I had seen in the hand of the man across the aisle. The 'short sword of the Romans' has never appealed to me. I would not like to have to use it. I like it less when someone else uses it. I got up again, and crossed the aisle. I said to this man, 'You will please give me the knife.' He said no, he would not give me the knife. I bumped him on the top of his head. He slid down in his seat. I said to the others,

'You will please get the knife and give it to me.' This one did. I threw it out the window, and sat down again. I was feeling very pleased with myself, and was no longer tired or sleepy.

When we reached Central, the man who owned the knife had recovered, and the Meridionali left the train there. I said goodnight to them, politely. The women answered me, but the men did not. At Town Hall the Australian was still unconscious, so I picked him up and carried him from the train. I said to the railway men at the barrier, 'Can you tell me please, where is a policeman?'

'Yer'll find one up the top mate. What's wrong with 'im? Drunk?'

'Yes.'

'Yeah, they're everywhere on Friday nights.'

I found a policeman directing traffic. I said, 'Do you please take this man?'

The policeman said, 'What's wrong with him?'

'He is very drunk.'

'Friend of yours?'

'I do not know him. He was on the train.'

'Should have left him there.'

I was silent.

'All right. It would happen to me. Give us him.'

I gave him the body, and the policeman walked away with him. Then I thought of something. I ran after the policeman and said, 'Excuse me please, can you tell me where is the bus for Kings Bloody Cross?'

He stopped. The man over his shoulder moved a little. The policeman put him down, and held him upright with an arm around his body. The policeman said to me, very politely, 'Where do you want to go?'

'Kings Bloody Cross.'

He looked at me silently for a while then said, 'How would you like to come to Central with me?'

'I do not wish to go to Central. I have been to Central. I left the train at Town Hall. I wish only to go to Kings Bloody Cross.'

'Where do you live?'

'Kings Bloody Cross.'

'Keep using that language and you'll go to Central all right. Into a cell.'

'How can my language make me go to Central? It is good English language.'

'Are you fair dinkum?'

'No. I am Italian.'

He looked hard at me. Then he looked at my very dirty shoes. He said, 'Give me a hand with this fellow. It's not far. Then we'll see about you.'

I said, 'Very well.' I took the man's arm, and we went down the street together. The man was half conscious now, and sometimes his legs took a few steps. Most times, however, they dragged behind as we carried him along. People were stopping to look at us. I felt embarrassed to be helping a policeman. But he seemed to be a polite one.

Outside an old stone building he said, 'Here we are,' and turned to enter.

I said, 'We are not going to Central?'

'Central Police Station,' he said. 'This is it.'

I suddenly understood, and wished to go away. 'Come on,' he said. 'Help me in with him.'

The man's consciousness had returned. He commenced to struggle, 'Not going in,' he said. 'Dirty cops. Let me go, yer dirty cops.' He peered at me. 'Know you, knives all over 'em. Bloody spy. Dirty cop. Free country. Not goin' in.'

57

The policeman took him in, still struggling and yelling. I helped a little. The policeman said to me, 'Sit there. Be with you in a minute.'

'There' was a wooden bench along a wall. I sat down. Opposite, behind a flat topped counter a very large policeman was sitting. He said, 'Gawd. Another one.' The man was taken away, still yelling. My policeman came back and sat down beside me. He looked at my shoes again. He said, 'Been working?'

'Yes, I commenced working to-day. I am a builder's labourer.'

'Are you now? Always work in shoes and a good suit?'

'I will obtain the correct clothing to-morrow.'

'How long have you been in Australia?'

'I arrived in Sydney yesterday.'

'I see. And where do you live?'

'Kings Bloody Cross.'

He thought for a moment, 'Who told you that was its name?'

'The taxi driver.'

'What taxi driver?'

I told him all about my arrival, and the taxi driver. He laughed very much. He said, 'Leave the bloody out. That's a swear word in this country. Its name is just Kings Cross.'

'I see. Yes. I understand now.'

He said, 'Come on. I'll show you where to get a bus.'

I felt very conspicuous walking up the street beside a policeman, but I was surprised to find that I liked him. He showed me where to get the bus, and even stayed with me until I got on it. We waved to each other. . . . I said to myself, 'Nino, nobody in Milano would believe it.'

Chapter Five

I T was nine o'clock when I wakened that Saturday morning. My shoulders were stiff, and some blisters were on my hands. Otherwise I felt quite well. A shave and a shower made me feel better still, and I went looking for some breakfast. I was much too late for breakfast at the hotel, so I returned to the Hasty Tasty. Then I went into the City, and bought myself some working boots, two pairs of shorts, and two khaki shirts. I thought about looking for a cheaper place to live, but decided it would be better to live nearer to the job. I would ask Joe on Monday. By asking questions, I found the G.P.O., and wrote a letter-card to my boss, briefly explaining the position, and requesting his advice. To avoid referring to the subject again, I will state here that he decided to discontinue my salary and expenses, and to pay me at casual rates for all articles and stories published. This seemed to me to be a very equitable arrangement. He said that if I ceased to become self-supporting in Australia, he would put me back on the staff again. However, that was later. Just now, I had posted my letter. I walked back to Park Street with my parcels, and got a bus to Kings Cross. I put my parcels in my room, and went out to gather some material for another story. There was very much to interest our readers at home, and I decided that what I observed, plus my experiences during my first day's work and afterwards, would be sufficient for the time.

I had spent nearly an hour observing the people, the shops and the transport around Kings Cross. The extremely casual and varied mode of dressing would make an article by itself, and I had many notes. Now I would relax, and follow my inclination until Monday morning.

Very soon it became my inclination to follow a young lady who was moving slowly from shop to shop looking in the windows. She had very blonde hair down to her shoulders and was made the way young ladies should be made but not often are. I thought she was beautiful. She stopped to look in the window of a jeweller's shop, and I stopped to look at her. Apart from looking at her because she was beautiful, I was making notes in my mind about her clothes, and her shoes, and the way she wore her hair with no hat. There were many people walking up and down with string bags and parcels and they were bumping into me, so I went to the edge of the footpath to watch her. There was a man standing there leaning against a car. He was watching her too. He said, 'Not bad, eh?'

I said, 'I do not know. Some young ladies are bad and some are not bad but it is not possible to discover this merely by observing them.'

He said, 'Smart guy, eh? Well, there's one thing yer don't know.'

'There are many things which I do not know.'

'I'll bet. I bet yer don't know she's a he.'

'She is a he?'

'Yeah. Or an it. That's a queer wearing drag.'

'I do not understand.'

'Don't gimme that. Mosta you blow-ins are queers. Wouldn't be surprised if yer one yerself.'

'Would you mind speaking English, please?'

'Wadda yer think I'm talking? Chinese?'

'Perhaps.'

'Orright, smart guy. I'll give ut to yer in words o' one syllable. That dame is not a dame. That dame's a bloke. Get ut?'

'A bloke? You mean that is a man dressed as a young lady?'

'Put it that way if yer like. Still interested?'

'This I do not believe.'

'Know ut fer a fact, mate. Her name's Charlie.'

'How is it that you know this?'

'Anybody hangs around the Cross long enough gets to know Charlie.'

'You are telling me that everybody knows this young lady is not a young lady?'

'Everybody except suckers like you.'

'Is it known to that policeman on the other side of the street?'

'Probably.'

'Why then does he not make the arrest?'

'Why do yer think?'

'I think he does not make the arrest because that which you are telling me is not true.'

'You callin' me a liar?'

'It would be more correct for me to say that you are mistaken.'

'I'm not mistaken, mate. Just givin' yer the good guts, that's all. Just lettin' yer know wot yer lettin' yerself in for. If yer too bloody pigheaded to take a warnin', yer c'n go ter buggery.'

'These words I do not understand. But there is one word I do understand. It is this word "bloody". I have been informed by a policeman that this is not a nice word. It is therefore my opinion that you are not a nice man.'

'Oh, ut is, is ut? Well I'd hate to tell yer wot I think o' you.'

'You have my permission to tell me.'

'That's big of yer. That's bloody big of yer.'

'If you continue to use that word I shall be forced to take action.'

'Take all the bloody action yer want. Go on, take ut!'

His attitude was most belligerent, and I disliked him very much. So I hit him on the top of the head with my fist. This caused him to assume a sitting position in the narrow space between the car and the footpath, looking surprised. But his expression of surprise soon changed to one of extreme resentment, and he began to swear loudly and started to get up, obviously with the intention to attack me. So I hit him again on top of the head, and again he sat down.

Our argument had brought a crowd of people around us and I heard a voice say, 'Don't hit him when he's down. Let him get up, yer mug.'

I turned to this voice, and I said, 'Kindly do not instruct me in matters pertaining to a private altercation.'

The voice said, 'Strewth. He's swallowed a damn dictionary.' Then it said loudly, 'Look out!' I interpreted this as a warning, but it was too late. Before I had time properly to face my opponent, I received a very severe blow on my right ear, which caused me to hear unnatural sounds, and to fall over. As I was getting to my feet, most indignant, another voice said, 'Here comes a cop.' The policeman whom I had seen on the other side of the road was between us, saying 'Come on. Break it up.' Much advice was given to him.

'Let 'em have a go.'

'Pull yer head in.'

'Why don't yer go home.'

'Garn, get lost, yer mug.'

'Give 'em a go.'

The policeman said, 'Break it up. Move along now. Come on, move along.'

Nobody wanted to move along. He took out a note-book and said to me, 'What's your name?'

'My name is Nino Culotta.'

'Where do you live?'

'I live at the Mayfair Hotel.'

He said to my antagonist, 'What's your name?'

'Mind your own bloody business.'

The policeman put away his note-book. He said, 'We'll find out up at the station. You're both under arrest.'

The man said, 'Like hell I am,' and started running very fast. The crowd cheered. The policeman chased him, and they both disappeared around a corner. The crowd dispersed, with many smiles at me. One young man said, 'Bad luck mate. Woulda been a good go.' I could not see the young lady with the fair hair. It is possible that she was what the man said she was, but I prefer to think she was what she appeared to be.

I decided to wait for a while because perhaps the policeman would come back and would wish to ask me questions. This he did after some time. He looked very hot and irritable. I said, 'It appears to me, sir, that you did not catch that man.'

'We'll get him,' he said. 'It appears to me that I'm surprised you're still here.'

'I waited because you may wish to ask me questions.'

'Did you now? Fair enough. What was it all about?'

'The fight?'

'Yes.'

So I told him I had only been in Australia two days and was not familiar with the customs. I told him as we walked along towards the Mayfair Hotel. He said, 'All right, Sir Galahad, forget it. But next time you want to fight for a lady's good name, go somewhere where it's quiet, eh? Not right in the middle of the Cross with me lookin' at you, eh?'

He appeared to be very desirous that I should agree to this, and I thought 'This is the second nice policeman I have met in this country. It is very pleasant to find two nice policemen in two days. Perhaps he will give me some good advice.' We were then on the footpath near the hotel, and I said, 'I am prepared to give you my promise that I will not fight again in your presence. And now excuse me, please. Perhaps you could suggest where I should go this afternoon?'

He smiled and said, 'First one that answers that gets sent straight back to the barracks.'

'I do not understand.'

'Didn't expect you would. Why don't you go for a swim?'

'There is swimming?'

'Go out to Bondi.'

'Oh yes,' I said. 'I have heard of this Bondi. There is a tram?'

'Not through here. You'll catch a bus over near the Mansions there.'

'Thank you very much. It is a good suggestion.'

'Don't mention it. And stay out of trouble, eh?'

I assured him that I would. And I said, 'Perhaps you would like to come and swim with me?'

He said, 'The way I feel now I'd go swimming with anybody. But I'm still on duty. Now go away, like a good fella, before I change my mind and arrest you for disturbing the peace.'

I went away as he suggested, and took a bus to Bondi beach. I put my elbows on the railing above the sand, and looked at the thousands of people lying there, and swimming in the water. The sun was strong, and there was a breeze coming off the sea. It was full of the smell of the sea, and I breathed it deeply. I thought how fortunate were these people.

There was a young man alongside me, with his foot on the lower rail. I said to him, 'I have heard that there are many sharks in this ocean.'

'Nothin' to worry about.'

'Sharks are nothing to worry about?'

'Look at that mob in there. Yer'd be dead unlucky ter be taken by a shark, with that mob.'

'To be dead is unlucky?'

'Wot I mean is the odds are about a million ter one. Yer'd be unlucky, that's all.'

'Can you tell me please, where is there a place where it would be lucky to be taken by a shark?'

'Funny bugger, aren't yer?' he said, and walked away.

That was two men who thought I was funny, and two children who thought I was not. 'It is because I do not understand the idiom,' I thought. 'Nevertheless, I will take a swim.' But first it was necessary to obtain the correct clothing. I said to another young man who was passing, 'Excuse me, could you tell me please, where I may obtain the correct clothing for the swimming?'

He stopped and looked at me for a moment, 'Say that again?'

I said it again.

'Hey Bill. C'm 'ere.' Another young man joined him. 'Say ut again mate.'

I obliged. They both laughed. The one called Bill said, 'Wot you want's a pair o' trunks. Hire 'em at the dressing sheds.'

'Where please?'

65

'Dressing sheds over there,' he pointed.

I said, 'Thank you very much.' As I moved away I heard one say, 'Place is full of 'em.'

The other said, 'Yeah. They're good fer a laugh, but.'

I found the dressing sheds and followed other people who were paying money to enter. I paid also, and entered. Opposite the entrance there was a counter, behind which men were attending to the people. I read the notices. Now I knew what the man called Bill had said. The correct clothing was called 'trunks'. I said to one of the men, 'I wish, please, the trunks.'

He went to a shelf and selected one, and put it on the counter. 'Towel?'

'Yes, please.'

A towel was placed on top of the trunks. 'Want a cubicle?'

'What please is a cubicle?'

'Place ter get changed.'

'Some person will change my money there?'

'No. I'll change yer money here. Place ter change yer clothes in.'

'Oh. Yes, please. I would like one of those.'

I paid him the money he asked, and he gave me a key on a pin, with a metal tag on it. On this tag was a number. He said, 'That's the number of yer cubicle. Leave yer clothes there. Lock 'em up, an' pin the key ter yer trunks. Got ut?'

I said, 'Yes, I have it in my hand.'

He said to his friend, 'Wouldn' ut?'

His friend said, 'Yeah.'

He said to me, 'Through that door there. Third aisle on yer left.'

I thanked him, and went through the doorway. I soon realised that the number on my key corresponded to one of the numbers on the many doors. The key unlocked it. This, I thought, was a very good system. I locked my clothes in this thing called a cubicle, pinned the key to the thing called trunks, and went out onto the beach. There were many people in the water, but they all seemed to be gathered together in big groups. This, I thought, was no doubt because of the sharks. I do not like to swim in very uncrowded waters, a shark would have no difficulty in finding me. But the young man had said they were nothing to worry about. So I determined that I would show these Australians that an Italian from the North was not afraid of their sharks. I entered the water where no one else was swimming. When I was about waist deep, I heard a whistle blow on the shore. I turned to see why, as it sounded like a police whistle. A young man with a close-fitting cap on his head, tied on with white strings, was waving to me. I waved to him. I had seen these young men on the newsreels at home. It was they they called lifesavers. They were very brave young men. No doubt he was saluting my own courage. At that moment, it seemed that the whole of the Pacific Ocean fell on the back of my neck. I was knocked down, and found myself on the bottom of the ocean, with my face in the sand. I got up with difficulty, in time to see another bank of water attacking me. I fought through it, and could see that there was calmer water further out in the sea. Once out there, I started swimming. It was very pleasant. The water was not too cold, and the sun was very bright. I floated on my back, enjoying very much the sensation of being lifted up and down by the waves.

Presently I saw another man swimming out towards me. And when a wave lifted me up, I saw three others on the beach, with their hands above their heads. 'Ah,' I thought, 'the lifesavers. They practise. They too are not afraid of the sharks. I will congratulate this man on his courage, and he will congratulate me. We will be comrades in danger.' The man reached me, and he appeared to be very irritable. He said, 'What the bloody hell d'yer think you're doing?'

I said, 'I am swimming. It is very pleasant.'

He said, 'Get over between the flags.'

'I do not see any flags.'

'Get over there with the crowd.'

'I do not like crowds.'

'New Australians. I've had 'em. You're in a rip, here. D'you want to finish up in New Zealand?'

'It is a nice place, this New Zealand?'

'You're goin' the right way to find out. Now get over there with the mob.'

'I like swimming here. I am not afraid of the sharks.'

'They're not afraid of you either. S'pose I'll have to haul you in for your own protection, you silly mutt.'

'What, please, is a mutt?'

'Look in the mirror some day. Come on, grab hold of the line.'

'I am sorry. I do not wish to play.'

'We're not playing. You're in a rip. Grab the line.'

'No.'

'D'you want me to use force?'

'If you attempt the use of force, I shall be forced to bump you on the head.'

He swam closer to me. I raised my fist to bump him. But I did not bump him. I did not know how he defended himself, but I found myself turned around, and he had gripped me under the armpits, and I realised we were being towed towards the shore. No matter how I struggled, I could not get away. So I soon ceased to struggle. I said, 'You are taking me to the shore?'

He said, 'Yes.'

I said, 'When we reach the shore I will bump you on the head.'

He said, 'We'll see about that.'

He took one hand away from me, and made some sort of signal. Before I could take any advantage of the situation, his hand was back again under my arm. Then water was crashing all around us, and I had trouble keeping it out of my mouth and nose. Then I felt that he was standing. I put my feet down, and touched hard sand. I stood up and said to myself, 'Now I will bump him.' He said, 'Grab him. He's trying to turn on a blue.' Three other lifesavers, whom I had not seen arrive, suddenly lifted me into the air. There were two at my head end, and one at my feet. My feet were higher than my head. They began to carry me through the shallow water to the beach. It was most undignified. I said so. They did not answer. I told them to put me down, and I would fight them all. Still they did not answer. They carried me up the beach, and the first lifesaver said, 'Take him into the club.' Despite my protests, and the curious people who were gathered around, they carried me right off the beach, and into this club. There, in the centre of a large expanse of floor, they sat me down. But they still held me too tightly for me to move. I was very irritable. The first lifesaver stood in front of me, and said, 'Can you understand plain English?'

I said, 'Is it plain English when I say I will bump you on the head?'

'Yeah, that's plain enough.'

'Then I understand English.'

He said, 'Good. Hold him while I read the riot act.'

He then proceeded to explain to me why it was necessary to swim only in certain areas, because of these 'rips'. He explained what a 'rip' was, and how he had brought me in because I refused to leave this 'rip', and soon I would have been far out, and the line would not have reached me, and there would have been much trouble. He was very polite, and I stopped being irritable. I said, 'I am sorry. I did not understand.'

He said, 'That's all right. Just keep between the flags. Everything all clear now?'

I said, 'Yes everything is all clear.'

He said, 'Good. Tell all your New Australian mates, will yer? They're a bloody nuisance.'

'I have no New Australian mates. I am only two days in Sydney.'

'Okay. See you around.'

'Thank you. I will see you around.'

I went out and leaned on the railing and watched the beach and the people, with this new knowledge in my mind. And presently I saw two men enter the water exactly where I had entered it. I ran down to the water and called out, 'Don't go in there, you silly mutt. There is a rip.' They did not hear me, and began to swim towards New Zealand. I waited for the lifesavers to come, but none came. Then the two men turned and swam a little way parallel to the shore. A large wave appeared and carried them to the beach. They walked up the beach, and I said, 'You are making trouble. Don't you know that there is a rip?'

They laughed, and went to sit down amongst the lifesavers with the coloured caps. I realised then that they also were lifesavers, who were probably not on duty. And I thought, 'It is all right for lifesavers to swim in rips, but not for anybody else. Therefore, if I wish to swim away from the crowds, I must become a lifesaver.'.So I went up to where they were all sitting in and around a canvas enclosure, and I said, 'Excuse me, please, what is the procedure if one wishes to become the lifesaver?'

They laughed. One said, 'Wot's yer time for the four forty?'

Another said, 'Can yer crack a wave?'

A third said, 'Saw a tiddler crack him a while ago.'

'You can't talk, you went down the mine yesterday.'

'Yeah? Wot about Maroubra last Sundy? All on 'e says, an' falls for it himself. Comes up blue in the face, spittin' sand an' seaweed.'

'I caught a boomer just after, but.'

'Who didn't.'

'You didn't. Out there like a shag on a rock, yellin' Mummy, I'm lonely.'

'I was waitin' for a big one. There was one out the back.'

'Did yer crack ut?'

'Didn't break. Didn't have me propeller with me.'

'There'd be a brown stain if y'ever did crack a howler, Bluey.'

'I'd be on my own anyway. None o' yous'd be game.'

'Listen what's talkin'? Be on 'im will yer?'

Not understanding any of this, I decided that they must be speaking the technical language of lifesavers. If I wished to become a lifesaver, I would first have to learn these terms. I walked away, thinking about this. Then I lay on the sand and went to sleep. I woke much later, feeling cold. Clouds obscured the sun, and a fresh breeze was blowing. There were not many people left on the beach, or in the water. I returned to my cubicle and dressed myself. Then I walked up the street. There were a number of cafés, and I decided to have my dinner at one of them. It appeared to be owned by Greek people. It was very crowded, and people were drinking beer with their meals. I found a vacant seat at a table where three other men were sitting. They each had a bottle of beer and were eating fish. I said, 'Excuse me, please. May I sit here?'

One man said, 'Help yerself.'

I thanked him and sat down. When the waitress came, I also ordered a bottle of beer and some fish. I did not hurry over my meal, because I was busy trying to memorise the conversation of my three table companions, and telling myself sadly that I would never understand these people. I will reproduce it as I remember it.

'As I was sayin' this bloke says 'e's a moral. Colossal times on the track an' Darby on 'im. Can't go wrong 'e says.'

'Best hoop in the country, the old Darb.'

'I seen 'im ride goats. Cooky too.'

'Cooky don' take on too many goats. Sharp as a tack, Cooky.'

'Wot odds d'yer get?'

'Twos.'

'Twos? 'E was threes in the paddock.'

'Makes no difference. 'E never run a drum, anyway.'

'Wot d'you 'ave on him?'

'Put a pony on 'im. Done ut cold.'

'Bob came out of ut all right, didn' yer Bob? Tin arse Bob they call 'im.'

'Done me shirt on the first, though. Shanks' pony 'ome, I reckoned. The old Cooky got me out of ut. Fifteens.'

'Wonder the stewards didn't 'ave 'im up. Last start at Warwick Farm 'e runs last at fours.'

'Cooky wasn't on 'im, but.'

'Shrewd 'ead the old Cooky.'

'Must be gettin' a bit long in the tooth now, don' yer reckon?'

'No longer than the old Darb, an' 'e's still bungin' 'em in.'

'Wish 'e'd brought this crab in.'

'Reckon 'e pulled 'im?'

'That's wot I reckon. But 'ow yer gunna prove ut?'

'Yer can't prove ut.'

'Somebody slung in a poultice, I bet.'

'They're all crooked. Man's a mug.'

'You'll be out there next Saturdy.'

'Not me. I've had ut.'

'Don' gimme that. You'll be there.'

'How did Bert go, did yer hear?'

'Still goin'.'

'I went all right last week.'

'That was last week.'

' 'E gets good information sometimes, the old Bert.'

'Sometimes. That was a good thing 'e gave me, the week before. Like hell ut was.'

'Ut was a good thing when 'e gave ut to yer. They pulled ut, that's all.'

'Ut wasn't pulled. Ut was dead.'

'Wot was the stable on?'

'They was on that thing o' Thompson's. Every one o' the bastards was on that.'

'How der yer know?'

' 'Course they was.'

'Mightn' a been.'

'I got two quid ter say they was.'

It was very depressing. I understood nothing. Yet my boss had said Australians spoke English, and he was a knowledgeable man.

Chapter Six

THE remainder of the week-end was free of language troubles. That Saturday night I obtained a seat at a picture show at Bondi. On Sunday morning I found St. Mary's Cathedral, and heard Mass there, which is the same all over the world. I lunched at a café in Bathurst Street, and then walked down to the Domain, where I listened to some very subversive speeches. These proved to me very vividly that freedom ·of speech in Australia was a living fact. There were many policeman listening, and they did not interfere even when one man declared that Bob Menzies and his party should all be stood up against a wall and shot. I visited the Art Gallery and walked down through the Botanic Gardens to the harbour, around to Circular Quay, then back up through the City to the same Bathurst Street café. After my evening meal, I walked up to Kings Cross, and before I went to my bed, I finished two stories for my boss in Italy.

Sydney on Sundays can be a very lonely place for a stranger who has no friends, and I was glad to be back at Punchbowl with Pat, on Monday morning. His ' 'Ow yer goin' mate orright?' was a very pleasant sound. We finished digging the trenches, although the arrival of a truck load of long steel rods held us up for half an hour. We had to unload them. They were very heavy. Two large loads of metal and sand were tipped at the front of the block also.

We did not see Joe. Pat said we would not see him until Wednesday. 'All 'ands ter the pumps Wensdy,' he said. 'That concretin's 'ard yacker. Anything ter do with concrete's 'ard yacker.'

But Joe arrived early Tuesday morning, bringing two large metal containers which Pat said were called forty gallon drums, and a smaller container which was a kero tin.

'We'll want 'em ter-morrer,' Joe said. 'Yer c'n use 'em for tyin' steel ter-day, Pat. Owyergoingmate—orright?'

'Orrightmate,' said Pat.

' 'Ow yer goin' Nino?'

'Orright mate,' I said.

'Good on yer mate. Ever tied steel afore?'

'No, Joe.'

'Nothin' to ut, mate. Pat'll show you. See yez in the mornin'.'

'Where's the wire?' said Pat.

'Gees mate, I nearly forgot. Ut's in the truck with the hacksaw.'

He got a roll of thin wire and the hacksaw, and gave them to Pat. 'Anythin' else yer want, matey?'

'Yeah. Couple o' four inch nails.'

'Knew there was somethin' I forgot. Bring 'em back right away, mate.'

'Orright. Give us a hand with these drums, Nino.'

Joe went away in the truck, and I helped Pat to put the drums where he wanted them.

I said, 'Pat what does it mean when somebody says " 'e never run a drum"?'

'Means 'e wasn't in the hunt.'

'There is hunting in Australia?'

75

'Racehorses, I'm talkin' about. If 'e's with the tail-enders, 'e never run a drum.'

'This is also a drum?'

'Yeah, different kind. We better get crackin' with this steel.'

He took a ruler from his pocket and measured a length of steel rod.

'Cut 'er about there Nino. We want a coupla dozen four foot lengths like that.'

'We want two dozen pieces, each four feet in length?'

'Yeah, you cut 'em. I'll go an' tee up a vice.'

He climbed over the fence, and I began cutting this steel. It was slow work, and I had not cut many when Pat returned.

'Okay ter use next door's vice,' he said. 'Give us wot y've cut an' I'll bend 'em.'

'You have to bend them?'

'Yeah. Use 'em for stirrups.'

'Is not a stirrup also on a racehorse?'

'Yeah. Different kind.'

I went on cutting, and Pat soon returned with some stirrups. They were like three sides of a square, with the ends turned over and inwards. They were all made when Joe returned with some four inch nails wrapped in newspaper.

I said, 'Joe, I would like to live near to this work. There is some place where I could live?'

'See wot yer mean, matey. That Mayfair's no good ter yer. See wot I c'n do.'

'Thank you Joe.'

We laid six long pieces of steel across the two drums, and Pat told me to cut up some tie wire into six inch lengths. He said, 'Now we gotta tie them stirrups on.'

'How do we do that?'

'Come over 'ere an' I'll give yer the drum.'

He showed me how to double the tie wire, and twist it tightly around the steel by using a nail.

I said, 'Are you not going to give me the drum?'

'Just gave ut to yer.'

'No, Pat. The steel is on both of the drums.'

'Showed yer how ter tie ut. That's givin' yer the drum.'

I said, 'That is yet another kind of drum. Are there many of these drums?'

'Plenty,' said Pat.

We spent the day making these long open boxes of steel to fit all the trenches. Joe did not return. My fingers were sore from twisting the wire.

Pat and I had two schooners of beer at what he called the 'Bloodhouse'. He said, 'Better turn in early tonight. Big day ter-morrer.'

'Yes, to-morrow we make the concrete.'

'Yeah. She's a bastard. Them mixers are hungry bastards. Toss yer ter see who goes on the metal.'

'You will toss me?'

'Yeah.' He took a coin from his pocket and threw it into the air. He caught it, and placed it on his wrist with his hand over it. 'Heads or tails?'

'I do not understand.'

'Ut's showin' a head or a tail. Which d'yer reckon?'

'Oh. I reckon it's a head.'

Pat uncovered the coin. 'Heads it is. You go on the metal.'

I said, 'Thank you, Pat.'

He said, 'That's orright.'

I did not realise how I had been tricked until the next day.

It was very hot that next day. We were all there at half-past seven, and there was a chorus of ' 'Owyergoin' mate orright?' 'Orrightmate.' We all unloaded Joe's truck. There were more shovels, a hose, and two large wheelbarrows with rubber tyres. A load of cement arrived, and we stacked it near the sand. Joe had an old wheelbarrow top, which he placed there also. He emptied a bag of cement into it. Dennis filled the drums with water by screwing the hose to the tap in 'the old chook's place'. The mixer arrived. It was disconnected from the truck which towed it, and we all pushed and pulled it into position between the metal and the sand.

Joe said, 'Who wants ter do wot?'

Pat said, 'Nobody wants ter do anything. Nino won the metal. I tossed 'im for ut.'

Joe said, 'Reckon yer c'n handle ut Nino? She's a bastard. Seen blokes keel over on 'er on a hot day.'

'He c'n start,' said Dennis. 'I'll take over when he's had ut.'

'Orright,' said Joe. 'You an' Jimmy on the barrers. I'll ram 'er, an' scram orf. You're on the sand an' cement, Pat, an' Nino on the metal. Twelve shovelfuls, Nino, an' no pikin'. Start 'er up, Den.'

The mixer was petrol driven, and Dennis started the machine by 'swingin' the handle'. Pat threw in three shovels of cement, a 'kero tin' of water, and six shovels of sand. Then he turned the bowl of the mixer over to my side. I started shovelling metal. Joe stopped me. 'No, Nino. Not like that matey. Yer don' walk ter the mixer from the 'eap. Wear yerself out. Chuck ut in. Here, give us the shovel an' I'll show yer.'

He took the shovel and threw the metal in such a way that it flew off the end of the shovel and into the revolving mixer bowl.

'Like that,' he said. 'Straight inter the drum.'

'That thing is also called a drum?'

'Yeah mate. 'Ave a go. Bung in another three shovels.'

My first shovelful missed altogether, about half of my second went in, then all of my third.

'That's the ticket,' said Joe. 'Yer gettin' the hang of ut. Bung in two more.'

I bunged them in.

'Fair enough.' He wheeled a barrow up to the mixer. 'Show yer how ter work the lever. Pull 'er out like this, then let 'er swing down. But 'old 'er.' The concrete ran into the barrow. 'Not a bad mix, bit boney. Then yer swing 'er over ter Pat again, an' 'ave a bludge while 'e's fillin' 'er up. Okay?'

'Okay Joe, I will try.'

'Can't ask more'n that,' said Joe, and wheeled the barrow away, with many grunts. Dennis walked behind him. Jimmy was waiting with the other barrow. Pat soon yelled, 'Right,' and swung the mixer over to me. I put in twelve shovels of metal, and did not spill very much, but Jimmy said, 'Hit 'er with another one.' Then he put his barrow underneath, and I worked the lever as Joe had showed me. The 'drum' was heavier than I anticipated, and some of the concrete splashed out of the barrow, because I let it run in too quickly. Jimmy said, 'Don' worry about ut, mate.' He shovelled most of it back in, and wheeled it away. I turned the machine over to Pat, and saw Dennis waiting with an empty barrow. I was panting, and perspiring heavily.

Dennis said, 'First seven years are the worst. Then yer get used to ut.'

I said, 'Seven minutes feels like seven years.'

'Stay with ut as long as yer can. Then sing out an' I'll give y'a blow.'

I began to hate that mixer. It was certainly hungry. The motor chugged along monotonously and Pat seemed to be yelling, 'Right' every few minutes. There was a growing stack of empty cement bags near him. Jimmy or Dennis always seemed to be waiting with empty barrows. Every shovelful of metal seemed to become heavier than the previous one. I took off my shirt. Perspiration was running into my eyes, and running down my chest and back. The waist of my shorts was wet with it. Small pieces of metal were continually getting inside my boots. Blisters were broken and sore on my hands. I was very unhappy. Then Pat turned off the motor, and the monster was silent.

'Quittin' time,' he said.

'Who sez, quittin' time?' said Dennis.

'Ah sez quittin' time.'

'Well ah's foreman. Ah sez quittin' time. Quittin' time.'

They both laughed, 'D'yer see that picture, Jimmy?'

'Wot picture?'

'*Gone with the Wind.*'

'No. Missed ut.'

'There was this mob o' niggers workin', see, an' one of 'em looks up an' sez quittin' time. Another bloke sez who sez quittin' time? This bloke sez ah sez quittin' time. The other bloke sez Ah's foreman . . . ah sez quittin' time. Quittin' time. Gees I laughed.'

'Nothin' funny in that,' said Jimmy.

'No sense o' humour, that's your trouble.'

Joe came over and said, 'Wotta yez all knocked orf for?'

'Smoke-o,' said Pat.

'Gees, is ut nine o'clock already? Time flies when yer workin' don' ut?'

Dennis said, 'Workin' 'e says. Squattin' up there with a bit o' four be two an' a level, while we bust our guts.'

'Somebody's gotta 'ave the brains, matey.'

'Takes real brains ter spread a bit o' concrete in a trench.' said Pat. 'Yer gotta go ter the Tech. Takes five years.'

Joe said, 'You gunna take five years gettin' that bloody tea pot?'

'No sir. Get ut right away sir. I'd do anything fer you sir. Yer know that, sir.' He climbed over the fence.

Joe said, ' 'Owyergoin', Nino?'

I said, 'Orright mate.'

'Bring yer lunch terday?'

'Yes.'

'Yer don' want ter polish them boots. Waste o' time. Grease the bastards. Mutton fat's the best. Best stuff fer yer 'ands too. Work 'er in every night. Keeps 'em soft.'

'You rub ut inter yer head every night, don't yer Joe?' said Dennis.

'No, matey, only inter me 'ands.'

'Thought sure yer rubbed ut inter yer head.'

'Wot would I want ter do that for?'

'I dunno. Something's keepin' ut soft.'

'Funny bastard,' he yelled. 'Hurry up Pat.'

'Coming sir,' said Pat.

We drank about three cups of tea each, while Joe told us about 'a bloke I 'ad workin' fer me one time—this bloke,' he said, 'was a chemist, see. An' 'e 'ad a beard. Reckoned 'e was trainin' fer the Olympic Games so 'e could win by a whisker. Said 'e was sick o' bein' a chemist, an' wanted the exercise. I give 'im a start. 'E was a good chemist, too. Fixed Edie up better'n a quack when she 'ad that poisoned finger. 'E stayed with me three munce, an' then pissed orf. Dunno where 'e is now. But this time I'm tellin' yez about we was buildin' a garage. She was an excavation job, an' we 'ad to underpin the bloody house. Clay, too. We'd 'ad the machine in ter take the guts out, but there was all this and diggin' ter get under the foundations an' tom 'em up fer the

F

brickwork. So I get some planks, an' make a run fer the barrer. Where was you then, Jimmy?'

'Earlwood.'

'That's right. Finishin' orf that job o' Smitty's. I give this Beard Watson bloke a mattock an' shovel, an' we get stuck into ut. She was a bastard down that 'ole. Hot as 'ell. I'm trimmin' the back face an' chuckin' the clay up the top, an' 'e's bullockin' in under the foundations, an' wheelin' 'is lot up the run. Goin' orright, too. Then I 'ear this bloody crash, an 'ere 'e is arse up under the run with the barrer on top of 'im. I thought 'e'd killed 'imself until I 'ear 'im swearin.' Pat thinks he c'n swear, but 'e's only a starter compared ter this bloke. 'E's pickin' 'imself up an' callin' the barrow everything, an' I told 'im, I sez, never 'ang onto a barrer, mate, I sez. Let 'er go if she starts, I sez. Better a broken barrer than a broken neck, I sez. 'E sez—I tried to 'old 'er. I sez, never do that mate, I sez. 'E says I didn' want 'er ter fall where she did. I sez don' matter where she falls mate, let 'er go. 'E sez O.K. We was diggin' fer about another 'alf hour, an' 'e sez wot are yer gunna 'ave fer lunch Joe? I sez—I got me sandwiches an' a couple o' hunks o' cake an' a bit o' fruit I sez. 'E sez—yer did 'ave. I sez wodda yer mean I did 'ave, I sez. 'E sez—ut was parked in the shade near the planks there where the barrer got away from me. I sez—yer meanter say ut's still under that bloody heap? 'E sez—could be. 'Aven't seen ut come out. An' 'e just goes on diggin' as if 'e didn' give a bugger. I shift the clay orf ut, an' y' orter seen ut. Flat as Aunt Maud's chest. Paper all torn an' yer can't tell wot's sandwiches an' wot's dirt. 'E says yer c'n 'ave some o' mine, I got plenty 'e sez. I sez yer know wot yer c'n do with yours, dontcher? 'E sez, I don't like ut that way, ut gives me indegestion. I c'n see the funny side of ut now, but gees, I coulda killed 'im at the time.'

'He was a good worker,' said Jimmy.

'Good as anybody y'd get,' said Joe. 'Bit slow, but 'e kept pluggin'?'

'Did 'e rub mutton fat on his 'ands?' said Dennis.

Joe said, 'I'd a rubbed ut on 'is 'ead if I'd 'ad any that time.'

'Like yer do on yer own.'

'Sling orf as much as yer like, ut's the stuff fer blisters. Keep yer 'ands soft, Nino. That's the shot. They're soft now, so you keep 'em that way.'

I said, 'Where do I get this mutton fat, Joe?'

'Get some from Edie. Always keeps plenty in the house.'

Pat said, 'Y'orter eat ut instead o' rubbin' ut on yer 'ands. Then yer wouldn't be so skinny.'

'Who me? I ain't skinny. Just in good nick, that's all.'

'Couple more nicks an' y'd be a pipe cleaner.'

'You can't talk. If yer was in the army they'd use yer fer a pull through.'

'How about a bit o' work?' said Jimmy.

'Yeah,' said Joe, rolling a cigarette. 'Better get stuck into ut.'

Dennis started the motor again, and we got stuck into ut. From time to time he and I changed work. He shovelled the metal, and I wheeled the barrow. Also I spilled some concrete when I ran over bumps. Joe said, 'Like me ter shift the trench for yer, Nino?' So I was more careful.

We worked on, and the sun got hotter and hotter. Dennis would frequently hose us and himself with water. Joe was singing to himself as he worked. Pat and Dennis were swearing all the time. Jimmy worked in silence; so did I. I had no energy to spare for talking or singing. I could not eat my lunch, and went to sleep in the shade of the fence. So did the others, except for Joe, who was talking to 'the old chook' next door. He woke us, when it was time to start again, and there was much cursing and groaning. It was hotter. Much hotter. Soon we looked like Zebras. Dust from the metal and cement covered us, and perspiration made striped marks in it. Dennis' hosing kept us clean only for a few minutes. It was wonderful to hear Joe say, 'Two more mixes'll about do ut.'

'Whacko,' said Pat.

'Bloody near time,' said Dennis.

'How yer goin' Nino?' said Jimmy.

'Orright mate,' I said. He grinned. His teeth were very white in his dirty face. I thought, 'I like this Jimmy.' We made the two mixes. Dennis wheeled the last barrow, and Joe called out, 'That's it.' Pat climbed into one of the drums, and stood in water up to his chest. Dennis returned and got into the other one. Jimmy pushed it over, and the water and Dennis both spilled out and seemed to spread over the ground. It reminded me of fish being emptied from a trap. I laughed. Dennis said, 'Wot are you laughin' at?' and began to throw handfuls of mud at me. I took shelter behind Pat's drum. I thought I would push it over also. I did. Pat joined Dennis in throwing mud at me. I rushed at him and caught him and threw him down in the mud. Dennis dived on top of us, and we wrestled in a tangled heap, until Jimmy turned the hose on us. He had a cigarette hanging from the corner of his mouth, and was not smiling. There was no expression on his face at all. We all laughed at him. Three small boys were standing on the street. They were laughing too. Joe came up, and said, 'Gees what a mess. Who tipped the drums over?'

Pat said, 'Them bloody kids.'

'Strong ain't they?' said Joe. 'Clean up an' I'll buy yez

all a beer. Y've done a good job. You too, Nino. Yer went orright mate.'

I said, 'Thank you Joe. You know what I reckon?'

'No. What?'

'I reckon I conk out. I reckon I bust a gut.'

They all laughed. Joe said, 'Mighta done too. But yer kept goin'.'

Never before had I been so tired.

He said, 'You'll be orright. Easy day ter-morrer.'

'Wot's on ter-morrer?' said Dennis.

'Gunna put that new front on Bill's place. You an' Nino c'n run the scaffolding up, an' knock out a few bricks.'

'Aw yeah,' said Dennis. 'Knock out a few bricks. Got an idea I've done that before.'

Pat said, 'Don' drop 'em on yer toe this time.'

'Droppin' 'em on yer toe's orright,' Joe said. 'Droppin' 'em on yer 'ead's the worst.'

'Yeah. Try not ter drop 'em on yer 'ead Den. Wot are we doin'?'

'You an' me an' Jimmy?' said Joe. 'Wheelin' in a few bricks. There's twelve thousand comin' here ter-morrer.'

'Gees,' said Pat. 'Drawn the raw prawn again. Face or commons?'

'Face. Commons are comin' Friday.'

Dennis said, 'Looks like you an' me havin' a good bludge ter-morrer, Nino. Away from the boss.'

I said, 'We will not be here?'

'No, I'll meet yer at the station quarter past seven. Show yer where ut is. Ut ain't fur from here.'

'Very well Dennis. I hope I am still alive.'

'You'll be orright, mate. Give us a hand to clean up, an' we'll go an' knock over a couple.'

'Wodda yer mean a couple?' said Pat. 'I'm gunna knock over a dozen.'

'Oo, you drunken common labourer. Are you not ashamed of yourself?'

'Yeah, I'm real crooked on me.'

We hosed down the barrows and greased them, and cleaned the shovels. Then we loaded them into the truck and drove down to Belmore. The first schooners disappeared as soon as they had been poured. Two more each followed rapidly, and then we relaxed, and the others began rolling cigarettes. I had some tailor mades, and offered them. They each took one. Joe said, 'Yer'll 'ave ter learn ter roll 'em Nino.' Pat took out his battered old tin and said, 'Here. Have a go.' They gathered around and gave me instructions. The final result was a cigarette very thick in the middle and very thin at the ends.

'Chuck that one,' said Pat. 'I'll roll yer one.'

He did so very deftly. 'There. Have a go at that. That's better than those things you smoke.'

I said, 'You are not sincere. You are all smoking those things I smoke.'

'Never knock back O.P.'s,' he said. 'Get yourself some terbaccer an' papers, an' practise. Ut's all a matter o' practice.'

'I will try,' I said. 'What is the best brand?'

'Log Cabin fine cut,' said Pat and Dennis together.

'Balls,' said Joe. 'That stuff'll kill yer. Ready rubbed's the shot.'

'Havelock,' said Jimmy.

'No, not Havelock. Havelock? Who the hell'd smoke Havelock.'

'I do,' said Jimmy.

'Yeah, I know, but who else does? D'yer ever see anybody else smokin' Havelock?'

'Anybody who doesn't smoke Log Cabin fine cut's not right in the head,' said Dennis.

'Well I don't smoke ut,' said Joe.

'See wot I mean?'

'What do you smoke, Joe?' I asked.

'Champion ready rubbed. The only smoke,' said Joe. There was a howl of horror from the others, and they all began talking at once, each convinced that only the brand he smoked was any good. Some men standing nearby joined in, mentioning other brands, and the discussion spread, and became heated.

Finally, I said loudly, 'Gentlemen, I have arrived at a decision.' They became quiet and looked at me. 'Each of you will make me a cigarette and I will smoke them all and decide which I like best.'

'Fair enough,' said Joe. 'Roll yer mine now. Good old Champion. Yer can't beat ut.'

'Yer got mine,' said Pat. 'But I gotta hand it to yer. Yer a shrewd bastard. That's one way o' gettin' back the smokes yer gave us.'

'Yeah,' said Dennis. 'Never thought o' that. Well, I smoke Log Cabin same as Pat, so that lets me out.'

'Yer reckon Log Cabin's twice as good as the other stuff?' said Pat.

'Course ut is.'

'Well you roll 'im one too, an' let 'im 'ave twice as much of ut.'

'Reckon I'm bein' got at somewhere,' said Dennis. But he rolled the cigarette.

I put them all in different pockets, and Joe marked

the brand on each pocket with a pencil. 'Now let's 'ave some steady drinkin',' he said.

With fresh schooners in our hands, we stood back from the bar, and Joe said, 'Listen Nino. I been thinkin'.'

'Did ut hurt?' said Pat.

'Pipe down,' said Joe. 'This is serious. Look, Jimmy's gettin' married on Saturdy. Him an' Betty's gunna live up at East Bankstown. Their own house. When they've paid for ut, that is. That'll leave his room empty at our place. How would yer like to move in?'

'Gees Joe,' said Dennis. 'Wot's 'e done ter deserve 'avin' ter live with you?'

'He could do worse,' said Joe. 'He could live with you.'

'Wot about 'im livin' with Jimmy an' Betty?' said Pat.

'Fair go mate, fair go. Wodda yer reckon, Nino? Four quid a week full board, an' Edie does yer washin'?'

I said, 'You wish me to live in your house?'

'Yeah, we got tons o' room.'

'That is very kind of you, Joe.'

'No ut ain't. We'd be gettin' somebody anyway when Jimmy goes. Edie c'n use the extra dough. No favours, mate. She's a business proposition.'

'Who, Edie?' said Dennis.

'You know wot I mean,' said Joe. 'Four quid a week. Edie'll cut yer lunch for yer same as she does now fer Jimmy. Are you on?'

'Am I on?'

'Yeah, will yer be in ut?'

'Thank you, Joe. I will be in it.'

'Good-o. Bring yer gear out Saturdy.'

'Wot about 'im comin' ter the bucks' party Fridy night?' said Dennis.

'That's an idea,' said Joe. 'We're 'avin' a bucks' party

fer Jimmy Fridy night. Cost yer 'alf a quid fer the grog an' the present. She'll be a good night.'

'How c'n ut be a good night without women?' Pat said.

'There'll be a coupla nines.'

'Aw well that's different. Women'll keep.'

'Be in ut, Nino?'

'What is a bucks' party, Joe?'

'Bucks only. No women.'

'A party for men?'

'Yeah.'

'No women at all?'

'No.'

'I will be in it.'

'Good. Cheers.' We drank.

'Dontcher like women?' said Pat.

'I would like to meet the men first.'

'Reckon 'e's queer, Joe?'

' 'Im? Not 'im! 'Ad one workin' for me once, but.'

'Who 'aven't y'd workin' fer yer?' said Pat.

'You, yer bastard. Can't say you're workin' fer me.'

'Now I resent that. I'm just the greatest little worker this side of the black stump.'

'Wodda they like on the other side?'

'Never been there. Cheers.'

'Cheers.'

'Cheers.'

When I got back to Kings Cross, I had a meal at the Hasty Tasty, and fell into bed and slept for nine hours.

89

Chapter Seven

Dennis was at the station when I reached Punchbowl the next morning. We walked to Bill's place. It was a brick cottage, with big cracks in the brickwork at the front. 'Subsidence,' said Dennis. 'That's wot 'appened in all that rain we 'ad last year. We're gunna put a new front on 'er. Two inch textures. All that timber up the side there's fer the scaffolding.' He shouted, 'Anybody home?'

A voice inside yelled, 'Yeah.' The front door, which was on a porch to the side of the house, opened, and a man came out. He was a big man, nicely dressed. He was not old, but he was completely bald, and he had no eyebrows. Dennis whispered to me, 'Looks like a boiled egg, don't he? But 'e's a good bloke. Mate o' Joe's.' Aloud he said, 'Hi-yah, Bill?'

'Hi-yah. Gunna make a start ter-day?'

'Yeah. We're gunna wreck 'er ter-day. Better start prayin' ut doesn't rain.'

'Won't rain ter-day. Paper says so.'

'Gees yer better take yer umbrella then. They're never right.'

'They'll be right this time.'

'Ain't yer workin' ter-day?'

'Yeah. Just goin' now. Been doin' the housework fer the missus. She's crook again.'

'That's bad luck. We'll be makin' a lot o' noise ter-day. Reckon we better come back ter-morrer?'

'No, she'll be all right. She's in the sun room out the back.'

'Okay, this is Nino, Bill, just started with us.'

'Pleased ter meet yer,' said Bill.

I said, 'How do you do? It is a very nice morning.'

'He always talks like that,' said Dennis. 'He's an Itie.'

'I'll keep ut dark,' said Bill. 'Gotta be goin' or I'll be gettin' the sack. See yer later.'

'Yeah, see yer later, Bill. Yer comin' ter-morrer night?'

'Bloody oath. Try an' stop me.' He drove away in a small car which had been standing in the street.

Dennis put his canvas bag of tools on the lawn, and took out a large hammer, the head of which was flat at each end.

I said, 'What is that?'

'Brickie's hammer. Three an' a half pound. Got a claw hammer here somewhere too. We'll need that. An' some three inch nails.' He put them all on the grass. 'You c'n start bringin' round those four be twos, while I knock in a few bricks.'

'Four be twos?'

'Four be two timber. Four inch by two inch.'

'Oh, yes.' I did some sums in my head, converting centimetres to inches, and saw what looked to be the size of timber he wanted. I carried a piece to the front. 'Is this orright?'

'Yeah, couldn' be better. Course, yer've'ad plenty practice.'

'This is the first time I carry such timber.'

'Yeah. Thought you'd learnt ut at the Uni. Bring 'em all round an' chuck 'em on the grass there.'

When I had carried them all, I saw that he had made a line of holes in the wall just above the height of his head. He said, 'Hold on a minute 'til I see wot I c'n dig up.' Then he went to the back of the house, and returned with a short step ladder and a mattock. 'We'll want the seven footers first.'

I did not understand.

'Four be twos. Seven foot long.'

I did some more sums and found the timber.

'That's right. Put one near each hole.'

He had now made a small hole in the lawn opposite to each hole in the wall. He put the claw hammer in his belt, some nails in his pocket, and placed the ladder near the first hole.

He climbed the ladder, and said, 'Okay stand 'er up.'

I saw what he meant and put one end of the timber in the hole. He took the other end and said, 'Now dig us out a pudlick.'

'I am to dig a puddle?'

'Not a puddle, yer maniac. A pudlick. Don't yer know wot a pudlick is?'

'No.'

'One o' these short bits o' timber. The shortest we got.'

I lifted a piece. 'This?'

'Yeah, that. Chuck ut up here.'

I handed it to him. 'Why is it called a pudlick?'

'How the hell would I know. Hang on ter that upright.'

I hung on, he nailed one end of the pudlick to the top of the upright, the other end resting in the hole in the wall where a brick had been.

He said, 'Yer know them long bits o' two by two oregon round there?'

'No, Dennis. I have never met them.'

'Well yer gunna meet 'em now. Them long light coloured ones. Bring 'em round. Want 'em for braces.'

'Do not braces hold up trousers?'

92

'Not that sort o' braces. Bring 'em round will yer, an' quit arguin'.'

I brought them around. He nailed one from the upright to the side fence, and another from the upright to the front fence.

'That'll hold 'er fer the time bein',' he said. 'Get the idea?'

'Yes, I get the idea.'

'Good. Well give us a hand ter bung up the rest of 'em.'

We bunged up the rest of them, and he braced them one to the other.

'Right round the back,' he said, 'there's a couple o' big ledgers. We want them next.'

'For the book-keeping?'

'Fer the wot?'

'Ledgers for the book-keeping?'

'No, fer the bloody scaffold. Gees you're ignorant.'

'Oh, what are they like, these ledgers?'

'Bloody great hunks o' five be twos. There's two of 'em up there. Near the planks.'

I did not know what a plank was, either, and realised that as far as these terms were concerned, Dennis was right. I was ignorant. These ledgers were very heavy. I carried one to the front, and together we put it on top and at the front of the framework already erected. He said, 'Drag the other end around while I skew nail this bastard.' I did so, and observing how he had fastened it, learned what skew nail meant, without having to ask questions. As we were lifting the second one into place, I thought out a sentence. I said, 'Chuck us the hammer and I'll skew nail this bastard.' I was very proud of that sentence, and expected some praise for it. But all Dennis said was, 'Good-o. I'll go an' dig up some tea.' He handed me the hammer and some nails, and went to the back of the house. I skew nailed the bastard.

Not knowing what to do next, I sat down and practised rolling cigarettes. When he returned carrying the tea in a metal container, I had destroyed many cigarette papers, but was able to make a fairly good cigarette.

We had our tea on the grass. I was looking at the work we had done now. I said, 'I think I understand what is to be done. We will put the things called planks up there, to become a floor on which to stand.'

'We will do that, man,' said Dennis. 'After which we will take up positions upon the said planks, and remove the bricks from yonder wall. We will cast the bricks upon the grass, whence they will be removed at a later date. Dost understand?'

'Indeed yes. When you wish it, you speak very good English, Dennis.'

'Oh yes, old chap. In my youth I was wont to conduct a plawstics factory in Keenyah. At a later stage in my astonishing career, I became a Colonel in the British Army at Poonah.'

'You are too young to have been a Colonel in the British Army, are you not?'

'Why not at all, my dear chap. I will be sixty-four next Monday month. My father will be forty-nine. He closely resembles the grand elliptical cesilical oozle bird, which flies around in ever diminishing concentric circles, finally disappearing up its own fundamental orifice, from which lofty eminence it gazes with mingled scorn and contempt upon its pursuers. After which it decreases in age until it becomes an egg. My father will be an egg on the twenty-sixth of January, nineteen ninety nine.'

'You will be over a hundred years old, and you will eat him for breakfast.'

'Egad. How horrid. Nay, nay, good sir. I will preserve him for posterity in a chamber pot. He will be pickled, which will be a condition to which he is not unaccustomed.'

'Pickles are very good with salami.'

'Salaam, sahine, salaami. Wilt not partake of les biscuits?'

'Thank you Dennis. I would like a biscuit.'

'Wouldst enjoy another cup of this fragrant brew?'

'Yes, please.'

'Well pour ut yer bloody self. Who was yer servant last year?'

'Last year I had no servant. I was living in a room at Milano.'

'How sad. Were not you lonely?'

'Oh no. I was very busy.'

'How doth the little busy bee improve each shining hour, gathering honey all the day from every little flower.'

'That is a poem?'

'Excruciating my dear sir. Excruciating.'

'I do not understand that word.'

'Neither do I. Is it not excruciating?'

'I know a poem in English.'

'Say you not so? I am enchanted. Speak on.'

'A garden is a lovesome thing, God wot.'

He observed me in silence, sipping his tea. Then he said, 'Wot's the rest of ut?'

'I do not remember.'

'Just as bloody well. Yer could get shot fer sayin' things like that.'

'Why?'

'Stand out in the middle o' George Street one day an' say ut. Bet yer get run in.'

'What is to get run in?'

'Ah, me. There we go again, this could go on all day. How's about bringin' round them planks?'

'The planks. Yes.' I stood up.

'Take the billy with yer.'

'Billy? He has gone in his car.'

'What the hell are yer talkin' about?'

'The man Bill. He has gone.'

'No, he hasn't has he?' He held up the tea container. 'See that?'

'Yes.'

'Ut's called a billy.' He threw the tea leaves on the grass, and washed the billy under the garden tap, together with the two cups, which he put inside it. 'Leave ut near the back door, an' start bringin' them planks around.'

We put the planks up. Dennis showed me how to knock a brick out, and how to leave every second brick protruding at the corners, so that the new brickwork would tie in. The bricks taken out were thrown down on the lawn. I said, 'This will ruin the grass of Mr. Bill.'

'Yeah. Do ut a lot o' no good. That's his worry. You carry on, Nino, an' I'll go an' build a bay fer the mud.'

I carried on. I felt quite important working alone. Also I think there is in every man a hidden desire to smash something. It gave me a great pleasure to break up that wall, and send the bricks crashing to the ground. I was soon covered with dust. I was very happy. But I did not neglect to observe Dennis, in order to find out what was meant by a bay fer the mud. It appeared to be a three sided box made of planks, held up by wooden stakes driven into the ground on the outside. It was finished when I had exposed all the inner wall of the house, down to the scaffold.

Dennis inspected my work. 'That's orright Nino. Bend them ties down, so Joe won't poke his eye out.'

Nino (Walter Chiari)

Kay (Clare Dunn)

Edie (Doreen Warburton)

Joe (Ed Devereaux)

Pat (Slim de Grey)

Dennis (John Meillon)

'I saw Sydney for the first time the very best way—
from the deck of a ship.'

Waiting on the wharf, Nino is told to 'get going'.

Nino books a hotel room (from clerks Barry Creyton and Bob McDarra).

' "Best beer in the world. Puts a gut on yer, though." '—Nino
in his first pub (with Jack Allen).

Joe (centre) introduces Nino to Pat.

'Pat said, "I'll start diggin'. You come be'ind me an' shovel
ut out." '

'I did not think I could continue to do this all day. My arms were losing all feeling.'

'I began to hate that mixer. It was certainly hungry.'

'Dennis dived on top of us, and we wrestled in a tangled heap.'

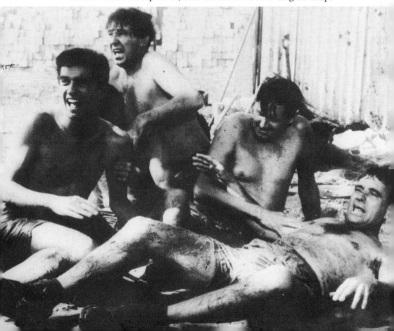

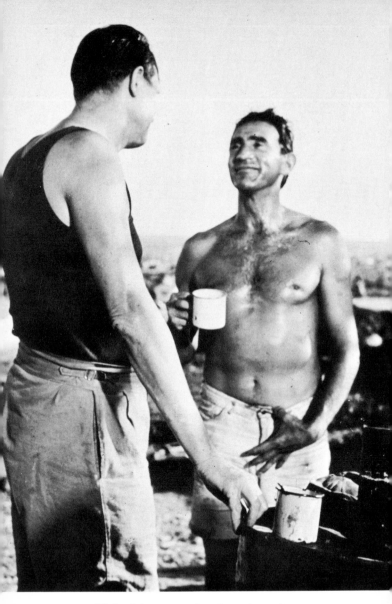

'He handed me a cup of tea. It was hot, and sweet, and very very good.'

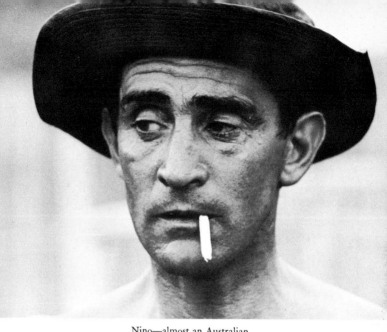

Nino—almost an Australian.

Dennis, Joe and Nino—mates.

'I was not
accustomed
to drinking
five schooners
of beer.
We were all
a little hilarious.'

'Dennis said fiercely, "One more crack about me mate and yer'll get one ground into yer dial.'

Nino and Dennis have a spell.

'I would show these Australians that an Italian from the north
was not afraid of their sharks.'

'They began to carry me through the shallow water to the beach. It was most undignified

' "Yabber, yabber, yabber. That's all they do." '—Nino and the drunk (Keith Petersen).

Joe, Pat and Dennis after their shooting expedition.

Edie and Nino

Nino shows Kay and Dixie (Judith Arthy) how to eat spaghetti.

Kay says no

Kay says yes

Kay's father (Chips Rafferty): ' "Wotta yer plannin' ter do? Dump my daughter down on a bit o' land an' build a home around 'er?" '

Nino and Kay celebrate their engagement with Dennis, Edie and Pat.

'Ties?'

'Them wires stickin' out. Knock yer eye out on them. Bend 'em down.'

I bent them down.

'Now we gotta wreck the scaffold.'

We wrecked it and stacked it. We continued to knock out bricks whilst standing on the ground.

Dennis said, 'She's gunna be a bastard when we get under the dampcourse. Bloody cement mortar. Have ter use the point.'

'Do not worry about it, Dennis,' I said, having no idea what he meant.

'I'm not worried about ut, mate. We'll get 'er out. Be a bastard that's all.'

It was. We rolled up the dampcourse, which was a long strip of lead. Dennis said, 'Joe'll probably bung that back in again. She's good fer another few years.' The bricks under it were cemented together. Dennis gave me a point, an iron spike with a flat head, and showed me how to use it. My right arm became very tired hitting this with the heavy hammers. The bricks were most resistant. Dennis cheered me by saying, 'She'll be worse when we get down ter the foundations.' However, it was lunchtime before we got that far, and the rest was most welcome. We washed ourselves under the garden tap, and Mrs. Bill came out in a dressing gown to talk to us. She was most upset about the great heap of bricks and mortar on the grass, and about Dennis' 'bay for the mud'.

He said after she went back into the house, 'Silly bitch. How c'n yer knock a wall down without makin' a mess? Women.'

'No woman likes to see her home in ruins, Dennis.'

'No, they want ut all prettied up an' smellin' o' polish

an' disinfectant like the Martin Place dyke. That's the way they want a man ter be, too. 'Ave a shave. Change those dirty old trousers. Get yer hair cut. They give me a pain.'

'They are very nice, sometimes.'

'Yeah. Sometimes. Not bloody often, but.'

'If all men thought as you do, there would not be any children. There would not be any people. The human race would cease to exist.'

'Bloody good thing too.'

'You would not have been born.'

'Another bloody good thing.'

'You do not really mean what you say.'

'Course I meant ut. Man's a bloody nuisance from the time he starts. Howlin' fer tucker, an' dirtyin' his nappies, an' gettin' sent ter school, an' doing everythin' wrong, an' gettin' belted. Then 'e grows up an' starts workin'. If 'e don't work 'e don't eat. Workin' an' eatin' an' sleepin'. Workin' an' eatin' an' sleepin'. Then 'e drops dead an' some other poor coot's gotta bury 'im before 'e starts ter stink. An' the bloody maggots get him, an' that's that. Wot's good about ut?'

'But Dennis, that is when a man begins to live. After he is dead.'

'How der yer know? Has anybody ever come back ter tell yer wot a lot o' fun 'e's havin' playin' a harp?'

'Do you not believe in God?'

'Look around yer an' see this grass. Growin' an' dyin'. Look at the animals. Growin' an' dyin'. Look at us. Everything an' everybody growin' an' dyin' an' bein' et by something else. If there is a God, He's got a bloody queer sense o' humour.'

'There is a God, Dennis. This grass—these animals. They do not happen accidentally. These hands with which we

98

work. They are wonderful machines. A man could not make them. The brain which directs them, and with which we think . . . what a wonderful machine is that.'

'Yeah. I know. I know. Ut's bloody marvellous. An animal's brain's bloody marvellous too, ain't ut?'

'Indeed it is.'

'Well I ate a coupla them fer breakfast yesterday.'

'I do not understand what you are trying to prove Dennis.'

'Not tryin' ter prove anything. The whole thing stinks, that's all. Don't make sense.'

'You would not expect an animal to understand what is in the mind of a man, so how can we understand what is in the mind of God. He is much further above us, than we are above the animals.'

'Why don't you hire a hall?'

'I do not understand.'

'Yer orter be on a soap box in the Domain. Ut's all bloody marvellous, but if we don't get the rest o' them bricks out, Joe's liable ter give us the sack, an' then we don't eat.'

'Why do you work Dennis, if there is only death at the end of it? Why not die now?'

'Because I like eatin', that's why.'

He maintained a gloomy silence as we worked during the afternoon, getting the bricks out with great difficulty. I too was silent. I lost my enthusiasm for smashing things. The afternoon sun was unbearable, as it poured its heat against the wall, and cement and brick dust joined with perspiration to make our eyes very sore. When the last brick was laboriously separated from the concrete foundation a few inches below the ground, we went and sat on the shaded grass at the back of the house and rolled cigarettes. Dennis watched me roll mine. He watched me light it. He watched me draw the smoke in. He heard me sigh with content as I blew it out. He said in a very gentle voice, 'Good?'

'Very good.'

'D'yer ever hear the story about the Irishman hittin' himself on the head with a hammer?'

'No.'

'Somebody asked 'im why 'e was doin' ut, an' he said because ut feels so good when I stop.'

'Yes, it is good also to stop after what we did this afternoon.'

'Yer supposed ter laugh.'

'It is not funny. I understand that Irishman. Happiness is the absence of pain.'

'Yer wrong there. Happiness is when pain stops.'

'Yes. I was wrong. That is true.'

'No pain, no pleasure. One balances the other.'

'I think that is true.'

'Reckon God invented pain because he wanted us ter be happy.'

'I could discuss that in Italian. It is too difficult for me in English.'

'Yer a good mate ter work with Nino.'

'I am?'

'Yeah, you am. When a bloke doesn't want ter talk, yer don't earbash 'im. Yer don't winge, either.'

'I am glad I do not winge. It must be terrible.'

'Don' know wot ut means, do yer?'

'No.'

He chuckled, 'Got a sense o' humour too.' There was a shout from the front of the house. 'Who the hell's that?'

We got up to investigate. It was a man with a load of bricks. He said, 'Where der yer want 'em?'

'Right there'll do matey,' said Dennis.

The man started to unload them onto the footpath. Dennis said, 'Hey, take ut easy. Those textures chip if yer look at 'em.'

The man said, 'Orright, I won't look at 'em.' He continued to unload them.

Dennis said, 'Come on, Nino. We better give 'im a hand. He'll break half the bastards.'

The man said, 'Thanks. I'm in a hurry. Got another delivery yet.' We helped him.

Dennis said, 'Not that way, Nino. Textures up.' He saw I did not understand. 'Don't stack 'em smooth side up. Stack 'em texture side up. Like this.'

I saw, and thanked him.

The man said, 'New Australian?'

Dennis said, 'Yes.'

'Reckon 'e'll ever learn?'

'He'll learn a bloody sight faster than you, yer dill.'

'Wodda yer mean?'

'If yer can't handle textures, yer shouldn't be cartin' 'em. Yer breakin' half the bastards.'

'Wodda yer want me ter do? Handle 'em two at a time as if they was eggs, like yer lame brain mate?'

Dennis leaped at him, a brick raised in his right hand. His left hand clutched the man's shirt. The ferocious expression on his face was frightening. He said fiercely, 'One more crack about me mate an' yer'll get one ground into yer dial.'

The man said, in a pained voice, 'Orright, orright. No need ter get shirty.'

'Lay orf 'im, understand?'

'Yeah, yeah. Orright.'

We continued the unloading in silence. Dennis signed the

receipt in silence. The man drove away, Dennis standing still and gazing sternly after him. Another truck arrived. The driver said, 'Where der yer want ut?'

Dennis said, 'In me hat, where der yer bloody think?'

The man grinned and said to me, 'Ut's the heat, gets a lot of 'em that way.'

He backed his truck up to the bay for mud, and tipped out a load of evil looking black stuff. It splashed everywhere. I said to Dennis, 'What's that?'

'Bloody black mortar. She's a bastard.'

He signed another receipt.

The man said, 'Hot, ain't it?'

'Yeah.'

The man winked at me and drove away.

Dennis said, 'No doubt about old Joe. He's a good organiser.'

I was silent. He said, 'Wot's wrong with you?'

'Dennis it was not necessary, the fighting. I was not insulted. If I am insulted I fight for myself.'

'Know that mate. Just needed an excuse.' He started to laugh. 'Gees, did yer see his face? He thought I was gunna kill him.'

'I thought so too.'

'Wouldn've touched 'im. Just lettin' orf steam. Now we'll clean up an' hang around 'til the loam turns up.' He was whistling cheerfully as we gathered up the tools and put them in his bag. Joe had said he was a moody bastard. Joe had said the same thing about Jimmy. I reflected that Dennis and Jimmy were the two I liked best. Perhaps I was a moody bastard also.

'Do you think I am a moody bastard?' I said.

'Wouldn't say that. Yer don't laugh much, but y'ain't moody. Why?'

'Joe said you were a moody bastard.'

He laughed, 'That's Joe. Not a thing in 'is head except buildin'. Says the same about anybody who thinks about somethin' else now an' again. He'd reckon you were if he heard us talkin' at lunchtime.'

'What is loam?'

'Gees you're hard ter foller. Yer jump about all over the place. Loam's just dirt. They get ut out along the river. Mix ut with cement, an' ut sets like a bloody rock. We use ut up ter the dampcourse. Joe'll probably only use ut fer backin' up on this job. He'll put black mortar in front. Looks better.'

I understood some of this, but did not ask any more questions. 'Hope ut doesn't rain. Bill'll get a nice wet wall if ut rains.'

'That will be bad?'

'Yeah, soak right through an' wet all 'is plaster.'

'I do not think it will rain.'

'Neither do I. Wot's the time?'

'Half-past three.'

'We'll give ut till four an' then shoot through. Round the back in the shade.'

We were about to sit down when there was another shout from the front.

'There she is,' said Dennis.

It was Joe, ' 'Owyergoin'mate, orright?'

'Orrightmate.'

' 'Owyougoin' Nino—orright?'

'Orright Joe.'

'That's the ticket, got 'er all down?'

'No,' said Dennis. 'Haven't started yet.'

'Time yez did. Well, how was she down the bottom?'

'Easy day, he says. Hate ter see ut tough.'

'Yeah, they c'n be bastards. Break many?'

'Most of 'em.'

'Don' matter. We'll use 'em up fer rubble. Need a ton o' rubble fer them steps on the other job.'

'Get all the face in?'

'Yeah, they're in. You an' me and Jimmy'll work 'ere ter-morrer.'

'Wot about me mate?'

'He c'n play with Pat up there gettin' the commons in.'

'Easy day eh?'

'Yeah, easy day.'

'Where's the loam an' cement?'

'Comin'. Got the gear on. Give us a hand.'

We unloaded the wheelbarrows, a forty-four gallon drum, kero tins, jam tins, mortar boards, shovels, and a thing called a 'larry'. We took them all around the back. Dennis said, 'Wilson's bringin' the loam?'

'Yeah. We won't wait for 'im.'

'Wot about the cement?'

'I'll bring 'er down ter-night, matey. Gotta see Bill.'

'Where's Jimmy an' Pat?'

'Down the rubbity.'

'The bastards. Wotta we waitin' for?'

'Nothin'. Hop in.'

We hopped in. I said, 'What is a rubbity?'

Joe said scornfully, 'Rubbity-dub.'

I said, 'Oh. Thank you.'

Dennis laughed, 'You'll find out wot ut is when we get there, Nino.'

I found out. Five schooners later I left, to a chorus of 'See yer ter-morrer matey,' and 'Don't forget ter-morrer night.'

Chapter Eight

PAT and I wheeled and stacked 'commons' all day Friday. We only saw Joe once when he came to pay us at lunchtime. He said they were 'goin' like a train on Bill's job', and they would, 'Drop the last one in this arvo.' He also said, 'Bring all yer gear out ter-night, Nino. She'll be a late session. There's no need ter go back ter the Cross. Yer c'n doss on the sofa fer wot's left o' the night. Move in ter Jimmy's room Saturdy.'

'Your wife will agree, Joe?'

'Who, Edie? Won' be there, matey. She takes orf to 'er sister's place when we 'ave a bucks' party. See 'er at the weddin'.'

'Very well Joe. And thank you very much.'

'She's right, mate. Want a hand with yer gear?'

'I have only two suitcases, Joe. I will get a taxi.'

'A taxi? All the way out 'ere? Cost yer the world, matey. Run y'in in the truck soon as we knock orf. Only take us an hour.'

Pat said, 'If that boneshaker o' yours c'n do the Cross an' back in an hour, I'll eat dirt.'

'Nothin' new. Look as though yer been eatin' ut all day. Orright, hour an' a 'alf. Be back before six.'

I said, 'This is very kind Joe but it is not necessary.'

'No arguin', mate. Pick y'up about arf past four.' He drove away.

'No use arguin' with 'im,' said Pat. 'Yer c'n talk yerself blind, but yer still do ut the way 'e says.'

It was nearly five o'clock when Joe returned. He called out, 'Yer ready Nino?'

'Yes, Joe.'

'Been sittin' on our dings the last 'alf hour waitin' for yer,' said Pat. 'Thought yer could lay bricks.'

'Got 'eld up matey. Dropped me level down the cavity. Took us an hour ter get ut out.'

'Yer always doin' that. Y'ought ter hang ut round yer neck on a string.'

'Hang meself if I do ut again. Hop in. Drop y'orf on the way past.'

But Pat decided to come with us, 'In case she conks out,' he said.

'She won't conk out, matey. Best truck on the road.'

'Wot road?'

'Any bloody road.'

'Alice Springs ter Darwin, if there was no one else on ut.'

She didn't conk out. We got back to Joe's place. Edie had gone, and Joe said, 'Dump yer gear in Jimmy's room. Unpack ut ter-morrer.'

'Is it possible for me to have a bath and shave before this party?'

'Course. Yer don' want a shave, but. There's not gunna be any sheilas.'

I had a shower and changed my clothes. When I came out of the room, Joe and Jimmy were sitting in the lounge drinking beer. Jimmy whistled two notes, softly, and Joe said, 'Gees, Nino, yer done up like a pox doctor's clerk. Yer don' need no coat an' a coller an' tie. Too hot, mate. Take 'em orf.'

I took them off. He said, 'That's better . . . 'ave a beer.'

He poured beer without waiting for my answer. I sat down with the glass in my hand, and said, 'There will be many men at this party?'

' 'Bout thirty or forty, if they all turn up.'

'Who's bringin' the niners?' Jimmy asked.

'Old Ned. Should be here any time now.'

'Who's doin' the supper?'

'Old Wong. Bringin' ut at arf past ten, when 'e knocks orf.'

'Long time ter wait fer a feed,' said Jimmy.

'We ain't waitin'. Soon as we knock these two bottles over, you an' me an' Nino's gunna get stuck into a pad o' fish an' chips. Edie left 'em. Only gotta warm 'em up.'

'I'll go an' start 'em warmin',' said Jimmy. He went into the kitchen.

' 'Ow yer likin' the job, Nino?'

'Very much, thank you Joe. The exercise is very good for me.'

'One way o' lookin' at ut. Yer doin' orright, though, yer worth yer chips. Gettin' on orright with Dennis an' Pat too, I notice. Couldn' say the same o' the last bloke we 'ad. Think yer'll stay with us?'

'If you will have me.'

'Good-o. Teach yer a bit about the game later on. Hey Jimmy. Yer beer's gettin' cold.'

Jimmy came in, drank his beer silently, and returned to the kitchen. Joe refilled his glass. 'Taught Jimmy all 'e knows. Got 'im top money in six months. Did five years apprenticeship meself. That was in the tough days. Anybody c'n get a job layin' bricks ter-day, long as 'e proves 'e c'n lay 'em, nothin' to ut only practice. Yer need speed on the corners. Give y'a go when we catch up a bit. Gotta 'ave me bath now. You an' Jimmy clean up that bottle. See yer later.'

He went to the bathroom. Jimmy returned and sat down. ' 'Bout five minutes,' he said, and proceeded to roll a cigarette. I did the same.

'Yer gettin' the hang of ut,' he said.

'Are you excited to be getting married to-morrow Jimmy?'

'Why should I be?'

'I should think I would be excited.'

'Been engaged two years.'

'That is a long time.'

'Yeah.'

'I understand your fiancée is a very nice girl.'

'Good as anybody y'd get.'

'You have the house ready?'

'Near enough.'

'You go for the holiday?'

'Yeah.'

'Where do you go?'

'Kiama.'

'That is which way?'

'South.'

'It is a nice place?'

'Good enough.'

I liked Jimmy, but conversations with him were difficult. I was thinking of something else to say, when he got up and went to the kitchen. He returned with a large plate of fish and chips, which he put on the floor in the centre of the room.

'Come an' get ut,' he called.

Joe answered, 'Comin' matey.' He appeared, clad only in

a towel, which was wrapped around his waist. He sat cross-legged on the floor. 'Bog in Nino,' he said, and took a piece of fish in his hand. Jimmy did the same. I would have liked a plate and a fork, but I bogged in, with the others. 'Help yerself if yer want some bread an' butter, Nino,' Joe said. 'Plenty out there.'

We emptied the plate, and Joe invited us to wipe our greasy fingers on his towel. Jimmy got himself some bread and butter and an open tin of jam.

'Yer good on the fang, mate,' said Joe.

Jimmy asked, 'Anybody want a cuppa tea?'

'Not me mate,' said Joe. 'Wot about you Nino?'

'No thank you Joe.'

'Wot we've 'ad ought ter hold us till supper time.'

'Won't hold me,' said Jimmy. 'Gunna make a cuppa tea.'

The sight of Jimmy eating bread and jam was too much for us. Joe and I had some too. And some tea.

'Knew ut,' said Jimmy. 'Just waitin' fer me ter make ut.'

'Never mind,' said Joe. 'Yer missus c'n make ut ter-morrer night. If she's not too busy.'

'They'll make ut at the pub,' said Jimmy. 'Two weeks.'

We ate and drank quietly for a while, then Jimmy said, 'Gunna put Dennis on the trowel?'

'Yeah, Pat c'n keep us goin'.'

'Wot'll Nino be doin'?'

'Diggin' out fer the garage.'

'Hard yacker.'

'He's used to ut. Done ut before, haven't yer Nino?' There was a shout from the back. 'Gees, the kegs. Youse get 'em set up. I'll go an' get me strides on.'

'Work ter do, so 'e ducks out,' said Jimmy.

The garage was at the back of the house, beyond a wide expanse of concrete, over part of which was a verandah supported on brick piers. There was a truck near the garage, and an elderly man in shorts and shirt and heavy boots was standing near it. He was a big man, with a big stomach, and he wore no hat. He was bald. He said, 'Where's Joe?'

'Gettin' 'is strides on,' said Jimmy.

'Wot's 'e 'ad 'em orf for? Don't tell me. Where d'yer want these niners?'

'Bench on the verandah.'

'Good-o. Give us a hand.'

'Nino—this is Ned.'

'How do you do, Ned?'

'Been worse.'

We struggled with the kegs, and got them set up on the bench.

Jimmy said, 'Where's the gear?'

'Bring ut when I come back. Bout 'alf an hour.'

'Coulda brought ut with yer.'

'An' 'ave you mob guzzlin' before I get 'ere? Like hell I coulda.'

'Don't yer trust us?'

'No. See yer in 'alf an hour.'

He got into his truck and roared away. Jimmy said, 'Builder. Hard bugger.'

Joe came out dressed in slacks and shirt. He looked at the kegs. He said, 'Ah . . . that's the ticket. Where's the gear?'

Jimmy said, 'Ned's bringin' ut back later.'

'Don't 'e trust us?'

'No.'

Joe said to me, 'Builder. Hard bugger.'

Jimmy said, 'Better set up.'

We followed him inside and carried out an enormous quantity of jugs and glasses, and put them on the bench. We got the dining room table out too. Joe said, 'Need ut fer the supper.' Stacks of plates and forks followed, and all the dining room and kitchen chairs. Jimmy brought a lot of boxes from the garage and placed them on the concrete. Joe said, 'Better check 'em fer nails.'

'Let 'em check 'em themselves,' said Jimmy.

Joe got a hammer and knocked in any nails that were sticking out. 'That's about the lot,' he said.

'Mornin' after,' said Jimmy.

'Gees yes, nearly forgot. Give us a hand, Nino.'

I followed him into the kitchen. There were two cardboard cartons on the floor, each containing a dozen bottles of beer. 'Grab one o' them,' he said. He picked one up. I picked up the other. 'This way,' he said. I followed him out the front door and around to the side of the house. He opened a small door which led into the space under the house floor and put his carton inside. I put mine there too. He locked the little door.

I said, 'Why do you do that, Joe?'

'You don't know these buggers,' he said. 'Drink everything about the place if the nines run out. Gotta save some fer ter-morrer. We'll need ut about lunchtime. Nothin' worse than the day after a do, an' no grog left.'

Men began arriving in cars and trucks. Pat and Dennis came over the back fence. I was introduced to everyone, and forgot most of their names. They all seemed to be connected with the building trade. The talk was all of building. There was an ironic cheer when Ned arrived with the gear, which was a pipe and tap combination for drawing beer from the keg. Willing hands fitted it to a keg, and jugs of frothy beer were drawn off and passed around. I could drink very little so soon after the fish and chips and bread and jam and tea. But recent meals did not seem to affect anyone else's thirst. In addition to the kegs of beer, everybody seemed to have brought bottles of some kind. There was beer in bottles, and gin, and whisky, and sweet sherry. The quiet conversations became louder, and there was much laughter and stories were told. It was a fine warm night. Somebody offered me some whisky—I drank it. Somebody offered me some gin—I drank it. Somebody offered me some sweet sherry. I declined and drank some more whisky. I began to feel very happy. I said to myself, 'Nino you must not get drunk. You are in a stranger's house in a foreign land, and you must not get drunk.'

Joe said, ' 'Owyergoin'mate, orright?'

I said, 'Orrightmate,' and slapped him on the back.

He said, 'Good on yer.'

It was a fine warm night. The conversations and the laughter and the cigarette smoke and the friendly faces were wonderful. The green grass beyond the concrete, where one went to eliminate surplus liquid, was wonderful. The big softly shining stars and the small fluttering moths were wonderful. Boldly I said to a man standing on the grass beside me, 'How yer goin' mate, orright?'

He said, 'Never better. She's a great night isn't she?'

'She's perfect,' I said. 'She's wonderful.'

'Yeah, them stars are right on top o' yer. Proper place ter have a party. Out under the stars. Better than bein' all jammed up in a stuffy room.'

I said, 'Yeah . . . how yer goin'mate, orright?'

'Never better,' he said.

Back on the concrete amongst the gathering of Australian men, I said to myself, 'How yer goin' Nino, orright?' And I answered myself, 'Never better.' I got a jug of beer, and I carried it around, filling up glasses. Everyone said,

'Thanks, mate,' or 'Good on yer,' or 'Wot about yer own?' I liked them all.

I said to Jimmy, 'I like all these Australians.'

'They're not a bad mob,' he said.

I said, 'They are a wonderful mob.' I went out to the bench and poured myself a whisky. I said to myself, 'Take it easy, Nino, or you'll conk out.' I made it a small whisky. Then I suddenly realised what I had said to myself. It was a shock. I stood still and thought about it. I had to tell somebody. I told Joe. 'Joe,' I said, 'it is wonderful. I am thinking in Australian.'

'Tough,' said Joe. 'Don't bust a boiler.'

'It is true,' I said.

'Good on yer,' he said.

I told Dennis, 'I just said to myself, take it easy Nino or you'll conk out. Not in Italian and not in English. But like that. In Australian.'

'No,' said Dennis, exaggeratedly, his eyes going wide with wonder. 'Not really. How marvellous old chap.'

'It is marvellous. I have never thought in Australian before.'

'In that case, old chap, we shall drink to this never to be forgotten occasion. Bottoms up.'

'Bottoms up,' I said.

We emptied our glasses.

I said, 'Let me refill your glass Dennis.'

'Not at all, old chap. Let me refill yours. What are you drinking?'

'Whisky.'

'Gawd.' He smelt my glass. 'Whisky all right. How many of these 'ave yer had?'

'I do not know.'

'Yer advice ter yerself was right. I'll get y' a beer.'

I waited for him, and thought that we needed music. We Italians love music. It combines so well with alcohol. In Italy, when there is wine there is song. There is much wine in Italy, so there is also much song. Most of us sing very well. I do not sing very well, but I do not sing badly. When Dennis brought a beer for me, I held it in my hand and sang. I sang, 'Viva Il Vino Spumagiante'. Not all of it, but some of it. Because I became aware that everybody was listening, and I thought, 'I am not a good singer and I am being foolish. I must stop.' So I stopped, everybody clapped, and there were cries of, 'Don't stop Nino,' and, 'Give us another one.'

I said, 'No, I am not a good singer.'

Somebody said, 'Better than anybody in this mob.'

Joe said, 'Good as anybody y'd get.'

Ned said, 'I'll sing "Old Man River".'

They abused him. They said, 'You're always singin' that. Give Nino a go.'

'Get yer mouth organ, Dennis,' said someone else.

'Right,' said Dennis. 'Hold 'im till I get back.'

He was wearing an old straw hat, upside down, and a pair of shorts. Nothing else. He slipped whilst climbing over the fence and crashed into the shrubs on the other side. There was a frightful shrieking and yowling. His head appeared over the fence and he looked very startled. There was a cat clawing its way to the top of his head. He was hitting at it. It leapt from his head to the ground on the outer edge of the concrete. It stopped suddenly and turned around and spat three times in Dennis' direction. Then it continued its flight, and leapt over the other fence and disappeared. Dennis, said, very violently, 'One of these days I'll murder you, you bastard.' Then he disappeared. Everybody was laughing mightily. Jimmy was rolling helpless on the concrete. I was fascinated. I had never seen Jimmy even smile before. He said, 'Funniest thing I ever seen in all me born days,' and rolled around some more. They picked him up, but he collapsed in their arms, holding his stomach. Somebody tried to get him to drink some beer. He couldn't. Joe said to him, 'Wot's wrong mate? Ut wasn't that funny.' They sat him on a box and hit his back, tears were running from his eyes. 'That cat,' he said, and bent in the middle again. 'Dennis' face.' He couldn't stop laughing. Bill, the man whose house we had wrecked, threw a bucket of water on him. Jimmy sat very still for a moment, then he stood up. We all watched him silently. He said, in a slow, quiet voice, 'Who did that?'

'I did,' said Bill.

'Did yer? Why?'

'Thought yer was gunna 'ave a fit.'

'Did yer? Well, I wasn't.'

He walked silently and with dignity, leaving a trail of water behind him, to the keg. Dennis came over the fence. He saw us all looking at Jimmy. His upside down hat was on his head again. His forehead and cheek were bleeding a little from the scratches of the cat. He said, 'Wot's wrong?'

A little man with glasses said, 'Bill threw a bucket of water over Jimmy.'

Dennis turned to Bill. His eyes were cold, under the ridiculous hat. He said, 'Jimmy's me mate.'

'We're all mates,' said Bill. 'Had ter straighten 'im up. He couldn't stop laughin'. Woulda busted something.'

'Wot was 'e laughin' at?'

'You.'

Dennis looked at him, unwinking. Bill looked back. Dennis walked over to Jimmy. He said, 'Wot was yer laughin' at me fer?'

Jimmy turned around with a glass of beer in his hand.

He wasn't even smiling. He said, 'Because yer was funny.'

Dennis said, after a moment, 'Well that's orright, then.'

He got himself a glass of beer.

Old Ned said, 'Get yer mouth organ?'

'Yeah.'

'Well give us a chune.'

'Go ter buggery,' said Dennis.

He and Jimmy walked silently through the crowd and sat on a box on the edge of the concrete. They sat side by side in silence, sipping their beer.

'Moody bastards,' said Joe. 'They'll come good in a minute. Wodda yez all holdin' empty glasses for?'

There was a general movement towards the kegs. Conversation commenced again. All about building. I no longer wanted to sing. Picking up the whisky bottle and a glass I went over to Jimmy and Dennis. I dragged a box up to them and sat down. I poured some whisky into the glass. Dennis said, 'Good on yer. Tip some in there.' He held out his glass of beer. I poured whisky into it. Jimmy held his glass out. I poured whisky into his also. We drank.

Dennis said, 'Reckon that business o' me an' the cat was funny, Nino?'

'Yes, it was funny.'

'Gees I got a shock when I landed on 'im. Thought all me birthdays 'ad come at once.'

'Never laughed so much in me life,' said Jimmy solemnly.

Dennis chuckled, 'Musta been funny orright.' He took his mouth organ from his pocket, and began to play softly. I did not know the tune. Jimmy beat time gently with his glass, on his knee. Dennis stopped playing to drink.

I said, 'I thought there would be a fight.'

'Coulda been,' said Dennis.

'Yeah,' said Jimmy, 'coulda been.'

'Know Santa Lucia?' said Dennis.

'Bloody Meridionali,' I said.

'Bloody who?'

'Meridionali. I do not like them.'

'Your privilege. Know the words?' He began to play.

'Yes. I know the words.'

'Come in, spinner.' He commenced again. I sang softly:

'Sul mare luccica, l'astro d'argento
Placida e l'ondi, prospera e il vento.'

Dennis stopped, 'Dat's good in Italian. Give us the words.'

He played a flourish loudly and began the song again. This time I sang loudly. Jimmy beat time with his glass. The others gathered around, and joined in, some singing words in English, some whistling, some just making noises. We were cheered at the end.

Someone called out, 'Wot about "Tiritomba"?'

'Don' know ut,' said Dennis.

I said, 'I know it.'

I stood on the box and sang it. Stamping feet beat out the time on the concrete.

'More,' they said.

I said, 'I will sing you a song that was becoming very popular when I left Italy. You will not know it. It is called "Vola Colomba".' I sang it. It is a simple tune, and Dennis was soon accompanying me. We had to repeat it. Then he and Jimmy stood up on their box, and with their arms around each other's shoulders, sang a song about a man at a dance whose trousers kept falling down. The song was a parody on 'Jerusalem', which I knew. It was called 'You're Losin' 'em'. It was very successful. They sang about a man with a big cigar, and a girl who went to Heaven, and 'Flip Flop She Flied'. He went to hell, and he 'Frizzled and

Fried'. Ned tried to sing 'Old Man River', but was not permitted.

The concert was ended by the arrival of four grinning Chinese carrying cardboard boxes of food. They were greeted with loud cheers. It was Chinese food, and very hot. It was chop-suey and chow min and curried chicken and rice. Joe and Jimmy and Bill filled plates, while others tried to fill the Chinese with beer. We stood around the table and ate with forks. It was very good. We ate it all. Joe said, 'Now fill yer glasses. There's a coupla speeches comin' up. An' while yez are fillin' up, Bill's goin' round collectin' subs. Ten deaners a head.' Everybody gave Bill 'ten deaners'. Then Joe called for silence. We all stood around with glasses in our hands, and Bill came to the head of the table. He had a brown paper parcel. He said, 'Yer all know why we're gathered here ter-night. We're gathered here ter-night because Jimmy's gettin' married ter-morrer. Goin' orf the deep end, 'e is.'

Cries of, 'Good on yer Jimmy.' 'You'll be sorry.'

Bill continued, 'Most of us 'ere have done ut. Some of us are glad, an' some of us wish we 'adn't. Ask old Wong there. He'll tell yer.' The four Chinese giggled and drank their beer. 'But we hope ut'll work out all right fer Jimmy. In fact we know ut will. They don't come any better than Betty.'

Cries of, 'Hear . . . hear.'

'So this time ter-morrer, he'll be an old married man. Worried lookin'. Yer c'n tell 'em anywhere. We hate ter see ut happen, Jimmy, but we wish yer the best o' luck.'

Everybody clapped their hands.

'Now just ter show yer wot yer mates think o' yer, we've all chucked in an' bought yer somethin'. Ut's not much, but ut's ter let yer know we're thinkin' of yer. An' we think yer a pretty good bloke.'

More 'hear, hears', and cries of, 'Open ut up.' 'Let 'im see wot ut is.'

'Yes, all right. We'll cut the cackle an' open 'er up.'

There was silence as he untied the string. He took out two objects. He held one up. 'This tape measure's a fifty footer. Solid leather case. We 'ad ter chase all over town ter get ut.'

A voice said, 'She's been oiled too, Jimmy. We run 'er out an' oiled 'er for yer.'

'She's a good measure,' said Bill. 'Never let yer down, so they tell me. I'm a grocer meself, so I wouldn't know.' He held up the other object, 'An' this trowel is . . . a . . . a . . . wot's this trowel Joe?'

'Weston,' said Joe. 'Thirteen inch.'

'Yeah. This trowel's a Weston. Thirteen inch. They reckon ut's the best yer c'n buy. I wouldn' know, but that's wot they reckon.'

'That's right,' said a big man with tattooed arms. 'Best yer c'n get.' He reached over and took the trowel. He bounced it up and down in his hand. 'Got a good lift on 'er. Pass ut ter Jimmy. Try ut Jimmy.' The trowel was passed to Jimmy. 'Try the lift, ain't she got a good lift?'

'Yeah,' said Jimmy. 'Good lift.'

'Well, that's about the lot,' said Bill. 'Except ter say that we're all thinkin' of yer, Jimmy, an' we wish yer the best o' luck.'

Cheers and handclaps, and they sang a song called 'Freeze a Jolly Good Fellow'. Then they called, 'Speech. Speech. Come on, Jimmy.'

Jimmy took Bill's place at the head of the table. There was silence again. Jimmy looked down at the table. He looked up, and appeared about to speak, but closed his mouth, and looked down again.

'Come on Jimmy.'

'I . . . er . . . er. I dunno wot ter say,' he said.

'Come on Jimmy. Give ut a go.'

'Yeah. Say anything.'

'I . . . er . . . she's a good tape measure. Er . . . thanks fer oilin' 'er. This trowel. She's . . . er . . . she's a good trowel. Betty'll think of yez too. I mean . . . er . . . aw . . . bugger ut. Thanks.' He moved away, embarrassed, amidst cheers and laughter.

Joe said, 'Well that's that. Now we'll get stuck inter that other keg.'

Chapter Nine

I DO NOT remember much about the remainder of that night. I remember much singing, and Jimmy saying goodnight, because as Joe explained, he had to be 'Lookin' good in the mornin'!' The only thing clear in my mind is Joe waking me the next morning. I was on the sofa, still dressed as I had been for the party. I felt awful. Joe did not look so good, either. He held a cup of tea in his hand, which was not very steady. He said, when he saw I was awake, 'How yer feelin'?'

'Terrible,' I said.

'Me too, if ut's any consolation ter yer. Yer got good an' drunk last night.'

'Oh. Was I disgraceful, Joe?'

'No, matey. Yer a good drunk. Singin' all the time. Get this inter yer, an' 'ave a cold shower. Come good in no time. We gotta go ter the weddin'.'

'I also?'

'Course. Don' think we'd leave yer be'ind do yer? Come on, matey. On yer feet.'

I got up. I felt worse. I said, 'Joe, I do not think I am able to attend this wedding. I am too sick.'

'Drink yer tea.'

I drank it.

'Now inter the shower, an' then come an' 'ave some brekker. You'll be right.'

I did feel a little better after the shower and a shave, and more tea and toast. I said, 'Where's Jimmy?'

'Went while you was in the shower. Down at the church waitin' fer 'is missus. Come on, we gotta get crackin'.'

We got cracking in Joe's old truck. He said, 'They 'ave Nuptial Mass in your country, Nino?'

'Oh yes. This is a Nuptial Mass wedding?'

'Course. Gotta do ut right.'

'If I had known, I would not have had some breakfast.'

'Forget ut. If yer 'adn't 'ad breakfast yer wouldn' be 'ere.'

This was probably right. We went into the church just in front of the bride. The priest was old. He was very slow. The church was hot. It was difficult trying to remain awake. Jimmy was assisted by Dennis. They looked very nice in dark suits, with grey ties. Betty was a small, well-formed girl with dark hair and large brown eyes. I wondered if she was Italian. I whispered to Joe, 'Is Betty Italian?' He looked shocked. 'Course not. Wodda yer take Jimmy for?'

What do I take Jimmy for? I take him for a walk. I take him for better or for worse. I take him outside. I take him away. I brought my thoughts back to the ceremony. The priest droned on. So also did a blowfly. I watched it. It landed on Dennis' neck. He brushed it with his hand. It came back. He brushed it again. It came back again. He covered the back of his neck with his hand. It landed on his hand. He removed his hand very slowly. The fly remained on it. There was a sharp smack and the fly was dead. Somebody giggled. Somebody else said, 'Sh . . . h . . . h!' Then they were taking Communion. Jimmy and Betty, and then Dennis and the bridesmaids. Then several people. I wished I had not had breakfast. Suddenly I became awake. I thought, 'Un momento. *Che* cosa?' Dennis takes Communion. I was remembering our discussion on God at Bill's place. Truly a strange man, this Dennis. I do not understand him. He argues that everything is nothing. Then he takes Communion. He kills the blowfly. One day God will kill him. One day God will kill me. I should not have had breakfast. I will not have breakfast to-morrow. I will take Communion to-morrow. With Dennis, perhaps with Joe. I glanced at Joe kneeling beside me. He was asleep. Or he was praying. His eyes were shut. I tried to imagine Joe praying. How would he pray? Would he use the language that was so hard for me to understand? God would understand it, of course. He would even understand Meridionali. Did God love Meridionali? God loved everybody. Even Meridionali? Even Meridionali. I should love Meridionali. Did God want me to? I said an 'Ave' for Meridionali. Perhaps if everybody said 'Aves' for them, they would improve. No, this was wrong. I should love them as they were, 'Love your enemies.' I said another 'Ave'. It was no use. I could not love them. I should not have had breakfast.

People were standing up. The Last Gospel. 'In the beginning was the Word.' What word? I had always wondered what that word was. As a child, I had asked myself, '*Che parola?*' I had asked my father. 'The word of God,' he said. I still did not know that word. One of Joe's words, perhaps? Indeed no. I caught myself smiling. I must not smile. The word of God. I must listen to the old priest droning the old words. Our ancient language. The language of my ancestors. No, not my ancestors. My ancestors were the tribes of ancient Gaul. The ancestors of the Meridionali. How have the mighty fallen? I must not think that. I must love Meridionali. This was the language of their ancestors. The ancient sonorous Latin. I was hearing it in a strange country, on the other side of the world. A country that had never

123

known Caesar. Who lived in this country when the Romans were conquering the world? The Romans had never heard of this part of the world. It was there, but they did not know. Centuries later, I came to it. I was a descendant of the tribes of Gaul, whom Caesar had subdued. Perhaps of Vercingetorix. Where are you now, Vercingetorix my ancestor? Do you see me here in this strange land where the short sword of the Romans was never known? Who were these Romans? Meridionali.

'Dominus vobiscum.' The language of Caesar. 'Ite, Missa est.' How would Joe say it? 'That's the lot mate.' We sat down, and I said an 'Ave' for Vercingetorix. And one for Caesar. And one for all the people who have died since man was made man. And one for myself, because I had eaten breakfast. The Mass was over. The bridal party were in the Sacristy . . . the people were whispering. Joe's eyes were open. They looked tired. He saw me look at him, he said, 'Come on,' and got up. I got up too. We bent our knees to the altar, and went outside. We stood in the shade of the church entrance, and rolled cigarettes. We did not talk.

The bridal party came out. Everyone was smiling and talking and offering congratulations. People were throwing rice over Betty and Jimmy. How ancient was that custom? That ancient tongue again. Women kissed Betty. We shook hands with Jimmy. He and Betty got into a car. There were white ribbons on it. Dennis and the bridesmaids got into another one. Dennis was between the two girls. He took their arms. He winked at me. A strange man. Joe and I got into his old truck. A crowd of laughing people climbed into the back. We drove off. Joe said, 'Well, that's that. He's done ut now.'

We went to Ashfield. The wedding reception was held there, in an old house converted for such events. There were waiters in white coats. We were offered sherry and whisky. The thought of whisky made me feel ill. I drank some sherry to be polite. The bride was late. She and Jimmy were being photographed. We stood around in groups and did not say much. Everyone was very polite. None of our building friends of the night before looked very happy. This I could understand. They did not look comfortable in their best suits. They should have been wearing shorts and heavy boots. Then Joe's wife Edie told me how happy she was that I would be living in their house. She said, 'I suppose it's a mess, this morning?'

Joe said, 'Don' worry about ut, love. Nino an' me'll clean ut up after this do's over. You comin' 'ome?'

'I have to help Betty's mother, first.'

'Good-o. Give us time ter clean the joint up. See yer this arvo.'

When Jimmy and Betty arrived, we all sat down, and waiters brought us plates of things to eat. We held them on our knees. Old Ned made a speech. He was very polite, and most unhappy. I thought, 'Betty is the only one who looks really happy.' When Jimmy was asked to speak he got up and said belligerently, 'I can't make a speech, so I'm not goin' ter try. Betty an' me are just gunna say thanks. Thanks.' He sat down, to much applause. The priest spoke also. He said what fine people Betty and Jimmy were. He said the bridesmaids were beautiful. When Dennis' turn came, he thanked the priest for saying the bridesmaids were beautiful. He said also, 'One of them knows this already.' She glared at him. I assumed that she and Dennis had had some sort of argument in the car.

Jimmy and Betty drove away. Everyone was very polite. I asked Joe if it was Jimmy's car. He said, 'No, mate. Belongs ter one o' the mob.' He and I and Dennis and Pat drove home in his truck. He said, 'Weddin's an' funerals. Can't stand 'em.'

'That bloody bridesmaid,' said Dennis.

'Wot 'appened?' said Pat, who was sitting on Dennis' knees.

'Ain't sayin'. Gees, I could go a beer.'

'Know where there is one,' said Joe.

We got it out from under the house. 'Coupla coldies in the fridge,' he said. He got them out, and put some of the others in. We drank them, they were beautiful.

The house was not very untidy inside, but outside it was awful. We washed the dishes, and brought in the furniture. Joe swept up the mess of broken glass and cigarette ends, and then hosed down the concrete. 'Gotta bury the bloody doin's, too,' he said. 'She won't last till Mondy.'

'The doin's' was the contents of the lavatory pan. He buried it in the back garden.

'Wot say we crack another coupla bottles?' said Pat.

We did. I was feeling much better.

Then we all went to sleep on the floor of the lounge, and woke up late in the afternoon, feeling irritable.

'Wot we need's another hair o' the dog,' Joe said, 'then a feed an' a shower an' we'll be right as rain.'

There was a note from Edie on the dining room table, saying she had been home and was going out again. She said, 'Won't be home to tea—you drunks can look after yourselves.'

'Wonder where she's gone,' said Joe. 'Not that ut matters. She's over twenty-one.' He was busy opening bottles. 'Bung on a feed, Pat. Plenty tucker in the fridge.'

'Bung ut on yerself,' Pat said.

'Give Nino a go,' said Dennis. 'Heard about this Italian cookin'. Wouldn' mind 'avin' a bash at ut.'

Joe didn't like the idea. 'Fair go, matey. 'E's only just come 'ere. Can't 'ave 'im cookin' on 'is first day.'

'Why can't we? Might be 'e likes cookin'. Can you cook, Nino?'

'Yes, Dennis. I cook spaghetti very well.'

'Spaghetti! Any bugger c'n cook spaghetti. Just bung the tin in a pot o' hot water. Do ut meself.'

'Oughta be half a dozen tins o' spaghetti in the cupboard,' Joe said. 'Dig 'em out, Den. I'll slice up the dodger. No hurry, but. Knock these bottles off first.'

'Have you any spaghetti, Joe?' I asked.

'Just said so, matey. 'Alf a dozen tins in the cupboard.'

'Not tins, Joe. Long spaghetti.' I demonstrated the length with my hands.

'Aw, them broom straws? Yeah, Edie cooks that sometimes. Oughta be a coupla packets somewhere, if they ain't full o' weevils. 'Ave a look in a minute.'

'Spaghetti,' said Pat scornfully. 'Gees, 'aven't yer got any decent chunks o' steak? Who wants that muck?'

'If yer don't like ut yer needn't eat ut. Besides, we mightn't 'ave any.'

'When will yer know?' said Dennis.

'When I 'ave a look.'

'When will y'ave a look?'

'When I'm good an' bloody ready.'

'When will that be?'

'When I've 'ad me beer.'

'How much beer?'

'Enough.'

'Enough? Looks like we'll be waitin' all night, then. Come on, Nino, we'll go an' find this spaghetti.'

'Right in the back o' the cupboard, if there's any. Wot's yer hurry?'

'Hungry,' Dennis said.

We found two packets. There were no weevils in them.

'What gear do yer want?'

'Gear? Gear is for getting beer out of kegs. I met this gear last night. We do not need it.'

'Gear is anything. Wotta yer gunna cook ut in?'

'We will need a large saucepan and some salt.'

'Comin' up,' Dennis said. 'Wot else?'

'That is all we need for the spaghetti. But the most important thing with spaghetti is the sauce. You should cut up onions and tomatoes very small, and cook them for a long time, until they become like a cream. This needs about three days. Then you should have some minced steak, and fry it very quickly until it is brown. Then cook it for twenty minutes in the onion and tomato cream. This is the best sauce.'

'Don't mind the twenty minutes, but I'm not waitin' three bloody days. A man's gut would be floggin' his back. Can't yer knock up somethin' quicker? Wot about chuckin' a tin o' stew on ut? Tin o' steak and veg, 'ere.'

He put a tin on the table. I read the label. I said, 'I do not know this, but perhaps it will be all right.'

'Good-o. I'll leave yer to ut. You do the cookin' an' I'll keep feedin' yer grog. How long yer reckon yer'll be?'

'How long will I be?'

'Yeah. How long?'

'About six feet. But I do not see why you should ask that question.'

'Strewth! I don' wanta know the height o' yer manly frame. When will the feed be ready?'

'Oh. The cooking will be finished in about half an hour.'

'Thank you, maestro. I will so inform the gentlemen within.'

'Dennis, there is a remark I wish to make before you go.'

'Make on, maestro.'

'I saw you take Communion this morning.'

'Woulda been blind if yer hadn't.'

'I thought you did not believe in God.'

'Now don't start that again. You get on with yer cookin'.'

He went away and returned with a glass of beer which he put on the table.

'Scream when ut's empty,' he said. 'I'm gunna 'ave a shower.'

So I cooked, and sipped my beer, and thought about Dennis. And I thought about the others, and how I would like to take them all home to Italy to show my people how strange were these Australians. Strangely profane and cynical and abusive, but basically such good men, delighting in simple pleasures. But I thought I would wait a little longer before sending home a general impression of their character for publication. It is not wise to make quick decisions about people, and perhaps disillusion would come later. I hoped not. I liked them, and wanted to continue to like them.

I was washing the cooked spaghetti with cold water when Joe came out to the kitchen.

' 'Owyagoin', Nino?'

'Orrightmate.'

' 'Ow's the scran?'

'The scran?'

'Yeah. Ready fer the nosebags?'

'I hear you talking, Joe, but I do not understand what you say.'

'Can't blame yer fer that. Don't understand ut meself 'alf the time. When do we eat?'

'The food is ready now. But I must apologise for the sauce. There is only something from a tin.'

I

'If yer got ut from a tin ut ain't sauce, matey. Anybody wants sauce there's plenty o' tomato an' 'Olbrooks there, but smells good. Dish 'er up an' I'll get the dodger.'

He cut and buttered thick slices of bread. We carried the food to the dining room table.

'Come an' get ut,' Joe said. 'Anybody want a cuppa tea?'

'Stick ter beer,' said Pat. 'Wonder 'ow Jimmy's gettin' on?'

'Wot's Jimmy got ter do with beer?'

'Nothin'. I was just thinkin' 'ow 'e likes tea.'

'Yer wanta cut out that thinkin', matey. Yer'll 'urt yerself.'

'Don't 'urt as much as listenin' ter you bein' sarcastic. 'Ow d'yer eat this stuff?'

'Watch Nino. 'E's an expert.'

He watched me. 'Looks easy,' he said. The first forkful fell back on his plate. 'But ut ain't.' He got some into his mouth. 'Gees,' he said, 'tastes just like stew with worms in ut.'

'Never tried that meself,' Joe said. 'D'yer have it often at your place?'

'Only when we got visitors.'

'Thanks fer remindin' me. I won't come ter tea.'

'Wait till yer asked. 'Ow d'yer know we'd 'ave yer?'

Dennis was saying nothing. I said, 'You're very quiet, Dennis.'

'Same ter you, mate. Good stuff, this.'

'You like it?'

'Yeah. Just what the doctor ordered.'

'Bloody crook doctor,' Pat said.

'If yer don't like the boardin' 'ouse, go to another one,' Joe told him.

'Can't afford ut. I work fer a builder. You know the lousy sorta wages they pay.'

'Yeah. Hard buggers.'

'Good pitcher on ter-night,' Dennis said.

'Where?'

'Local flea house.'

'Wot is ut?'

'*Men from Mars.*'

'Kook-kook-kook-kook-kook,' said Pat.

'Wodda yer tryin' ter do? Lay an egg?'

'Men from Mars. That's wot they say. Kook-kook-kook-kook-kook.'

'Don' make sense,' Joe said.

'Reckon wot you say wouldn' make sense to them, either.'

'Yer goin', Den?'

'You bet. Space men. Roll their eyes an' shoot yer dead with invisible rays. Thrilling. Super-colossal. Adults only. Four bob upstairs.'

'That dame goin'?'

'Wot dame?'

'That black-haired one you had last Sat'dy night.'

'Could be. Wot's ut to yer?'

'Nothin'. Just wonderin'.'

'Well, quit wonderin'. Anybody comin'?'

'Not if yer goin' with 'er.'

'Who says I'm goin' with her? Did I say I'm goin' with her?'

'Orright. Orright. Don't fall orf.'

'Who's fallin' orf? Just askin' is anybody comin'.' He took another piece of buttered bread. 'Wot about you, Nino?'

'No thank you, Dennis. I have had sufficient, thank you.'

This simple answer provoked very loud laughter. I was

surprised. I said: 'It is not funny. I was hungry, and now I have had enough.'

'I've had more than e-bloody-nough,' said Pat. 'Yer all bats.'

'Nino,' said Dennis very sweetly.

'Yes, Dennis?'

'It is my intention to visit the local picture palace this evening, to view therein a show entitled *Men from Mars*. Wouldst care to accompany me?'

'Thank you, Dennis. I will be very pleased to accompany you.'

'One sucker in,' Pat said.

Joe appeared interested. 'You shoutin'?'

'Yankee shout,' said Dennis.

'If there is to be shouting,' I said, 'perhaps I had better not go. I have had sufficient beer.'

'That'll be the day when you get beer at the pitchers.'

'Better than ice cream an' chocolates.'

'Ever notice,' Joe said, 'whenever yer take yer missus ter the pitchers, she wants an ice cream? Never thinks of ut any other time.'

'How would we notice that? We ain't married.'

'Aw, tha's right. Keep fergettin'. Yez look married.'

'That comes from workin' fer you. Wot time's Edie comin' home?'

'How would I know? Don't even know where she is.'

'Well, wot about comin' ter the flicks?'

'Might as well. Be in ut, Nino?'

'Whatever it is I will be in it, Joe.'

'Good-o. We'll wash up an' scrape off the whiskers an' knock over a few more bottles before we go, eh? Best part of a dozen still left. Decent feed, Nino. Yer c'd get a job as a shearers' cook any time.'

'They'd all go on strike,' Pat said.

'I hate sheep,' Dennis said. 'Stupid bastards.'

'You was a jackeroo once, wasn't you, Den?'

'Yeah. Walgett. Nothin' worse.'

'Worse than layin' bricks?'

'Yeah.'

'Must a bin crook, then.'

'Sheep! Worse than bloody turkeys.'

Pat said, 'Seen a mob o' turkeys tryin' ter get out through a nail hole in a tin shed once. Killed 'emselves.'

'Yeah,' said Dennis, 'a hawk c'n come an' pinch all their young uns, an' they take no notice. Bit o' paper blows along the ground an' they get the tom tits an' fly into a fence an' knock 'emselves cold. They have turkeys in Italy, Nino?'

'Yes, Dennis.'

'Y'ain't sayin' much. Wot's the matter, mate? Tired?'

'No. I am not tired.'

'Keepin' awful quiet.'

'I am sure the conversation is very interesting, but unfortunately I cannot understand it.'

'Y'ain't missed much,' Joe said. 'Come on. Let's wash up.'

We washed the dishes and bathed and shaved, and I listened to Joe's radio while he and the others drank more beer. I could not drink more beer. Then we went down to the picture show. Dennis and Pat made noises of ironic appreciation throughout the show, and many people told them to keep quiet. We walked back in the moonlight and they came into Joe's house for some supper. This was a loaf of bread made into toast, and coffee made with milk instead of water. I had not previously tasted this, and found it very good. Edie was home. She had some supper with us, talking about the people she had visited. Joe said they were a 'lot o' dills'. Edie resented this remark and they had an argument. She said they were nicer people than *his* friends, and he said did she mean present company? She said 'present company excepted', and Joe said 'just as bloody well'. She objected to his swearing, and Joe said 'bloody' was not swearing, and I said a policeman had told me that 'bloody' was not a nice word. Joe said the policeman was a 'dill' and Pat and Dennis supported him, and Edie said she was glad I had a policeman friend, because the New South Wales police were the best in the world. Joe wanted to know how she knew this when she had never seen any other kind and she said she had read it in a magazine, and Joe said 'bloody read ut in the *Women's Weekly*, I s'pose'. Edie again objected to his use of the word 'bloody', and Joe said he was sick of bloody women tryin' ter teach him how ter talk, and Edie asked why couldn't he learn to speak nicely like Nino. Dennis and Pat began to imitate my speech in an exaggerated manner.

'I say, old chap, would you mind passing me another slice of that excellent toast?'

'Not at all, old man. I always think that toast refreshes one, do not you?'

'Indubitably. Indubitably. But I must say the coffee is superb.'

'Superb, my dear fellow, is an understatement. It is elegant. Only the sublime technique of our kindly host could produce such a delectable beverage.'

'No doubt he acquired the knowledge from his charming spouse.'

'No doubt whatsoever. No doubt at all. Isn't the weather shocking?'

'Appalling, my dear chap, appalling. I was only saying to Cholmondeley the other day—the weather is appalling. He agreed with me. Good chap Cholmondeley.'

'Wasn't his father one of the Cholmondeleys of——?'

'Indeed, yes. Yes, indeed. Married Felicia Fetherston-haugh, you know.'

'Charming girl, charming.'

'Yes, indeed.'

'Dennis,' I said, 'why do you not speak good English always?'

'Man'd feel a prawn. Got another cuppa mud, Joe?'

'Sure,' Joe said. 'Chuck us yer empty.'

Edie said, 'I'm going to bed. You're all mad. It's impossible to get any sense out of you. Goodnight, Nino.'

'Goodnight, Edie.'

'Hey,' Joe said, 'wot about goodnight ter yer old man?' She ruffled his hair. 'Goodnight, you bloody fool,' she said. ' 'Night, Dennis. 'Night, Pat.'

' 'Night,' they said.

'That's me missus,' Joe said, 'never a cross word.'

'Wodda we doin' ter-morrer?' said Pat.

'It's ter-morrer now,' Dennis told him.

'Orright, wodda we doin' ter-day?'

'Know wot I'd like ter do?' Joe said.

'Wot?'

'Go shootin'.'

'I'll be in that,' said Pat. 'Where'll we go?'

'Got an idea,' Dennis said. 'Use yer phone, Joe?'

'Go ahead, matey.'

Dennis went to the phone in the small hall near the front door, and Joe told me of the joys of shooting. I understood the theme but not the details. Dennis came back.

'I did real good,' he said. 'Stanwell Park. Paper train leaves in a coupla hours. We c'n do ut easy.'

'Pick ut up at Sydenham,' said Joe.

'Got time ter go right into Central. Get a seat.'

'Yeah. Still got that japara tent o' yours, Dennis?'

'Course I still got ut. Think I'd give ut away?'

'Then 'ow we orf for ammo?'

'I got fifty,' said Dennis.

'Me too,' said Pat.

'We're jake, then. Chuck some tucker into a pack an' get crackin', eh?'

'Tucker's on us,' Dennis said. 'You bin turnin' ut on long enough.'

'Won't argue,' Joe said. 'You get organised an' I'll go an' square orf with Edie.'

'Might be asleep.'

'Wake 'er up.'

'Might be dangerous.'

'Couldn't care less, matey. Wait there, Nino. We're goin' shootin'. Show yer a bit o' bush.'

Dennis and Pat went out the back door. Joe went into the front bedroom. I listened to popular music from station 2UW, not at all certain of what was intended. Joe was the first to come back.

'All set, matey. She went a bit crook, but she'll be sweet.'

'Joe,' I said. 'I do not fully understand what is it exactly that we are going to do. And please, do not speak Australian.'

'Wot else c'n a bloke speak? All right, I'll make it simple. We're goin' down to a place called Stanwell Park and we've got rifles an' ammunition, an' we're goin' shootin'.'

'What do we shoot?'

'Rabbits mostly. Maybe pigeons. She'll be a good day!'

'We do not go to bed?'

'Sleep in the train. We'll get there before daylight. Sleep

136

a coupla hours in the tent if we want. She'll be a good day
Wodda yer like with a rifle? Can yer shoot?'

'I do not know much about this shooting.'

'You'll learn matey. You'll learn. Nothin' to ut. Wot
about another cuppa coffee?'

Chapter Ten

EDIE came out wearing a dressing gown.

'I think you're all mad,' she said. 'And what about that grass? You were going to cut the grass to-morrow.'

'She'll keep fer another week,' Joe told her.

'It's nearly up to my knees now. I won't be able to find the clothes line soon.'

'Lend y'a compass. Don't worry about ut, mate. Cut ut next week-end fer sure.'

'That's what you said last week-end.'

'Orright, orright. Didn't know we'd be havin' Nino. Gotta look after 'im. Next week-end fer sure, mate.'

'That's right, blame it on Nino.'

'Gotta blame ut on somebody. Can't blame ut on meself.'

'Of course, *you* don't *want* to go shooting, do you?'

'Not perticlerly. Sooner cut the grass. Can't let Nino go by himself, but. 'E'd get lorst.'

'What about Pat and Dennis?'

'They'd get lorst quicker'n Nino. No, mate, gotta go and look after 'em. Why'n't yer come with us?'

'I'm not that stupid,' said Edie. 'Paper train! If you must go, why don't you take the truck?'

'Can't take the risk o' bein' held up. She's about due ter conk out.'

Edie went back to bed and Joe grinned, saying: 'Joys o' married life. Come on. Get inta our old workin' togs.'

We were ready when Dennis and Pat came in, with a rolled-up tent, two rifles and a well-filled pack.

'Gees,' said Joe, 'is that all tucker?'

'Yer get hungry when yer shootin'.'

'Wot's wrong with cookin' a few rabbits?'

'Mightn't get any.'

'That's wot I like about you, matey. Always cheerful. Wot time's the next train ter Central?'

'Ain't a clue.'

'Well, ring up an' find out.'

'Buggers down there wouldn' 'ave a clue either. Yez ready?'

'Yeah. Just get me rifle.'

Pat said: 'You're the biggest, Nino. You c'n carry the pack.'

The man in the ticket office at the station said we were mad too, and Dennis said 'Kook-kook-kook-kook-kook' to him. He and Pat played Men from Mars all the way to Central.

The paper train was crowded with men and Boy Scouts. We found seats at the end of a carriage. Many of the men were drunk. Joe said they were 'coal miners arrivin' back from a spree'. Most of them were singing mournfully and did not appear to be very happy. The train stopped for long periods at small stations while men shouted at each other, doors banged, bundles of papers thudded onto the platform and Boy Scouts, curled up like pups, slept peacefully. Joe and Dennis and Pat, with their hats over their eyes and their legs stretched out in front of them, also slept. But I was wakeful, listening to the noises of the night, to the wailing songs, and watching the singers. Two men in a seat across the aisle snored loudly on each other's shoulders. An argument started at the other end of the carriage.

'I tell y' it's 'ere somewhere.'

'Well, hurry up. I can't wait all night.'

' 'Ad ut in me pocket. Know I did. Put ut in with me 'alf a quid.'

'Why isn't it there now?'

' 'Ow do I know ? Ut *was* there.'

'You'll have to pay excess fare.'

'Aw, use yer skull. 'Ow c'n I pay excess fare when I on'y got 'alf a quid? 'Ow can I, eh?'

'I'll have to take your name and address.'

'Now don' be 'ard ter get on with. 'Ang on till I 'ave another look. Ut's 'ere somewhere. Know ut is.'

One of the sleeping men opposite me woke up.

'Gees,' he said, 'ut's me mate.'

He stood up and lurched along the aisle. He was a small man who badly needed a shave. I heard his voice say, 'Wot's the matter, love?'

'Can't find me bloody ticket.'

'Well, never mind, love. Yer got ut somewhere. Where'd yer put ut?'

'In with me 'alf a quid.'

'Sure yer didn' put ut in yer 'at?'

'Course I'm sure. Put ut in with me 'alf a quid.'

'Where's yer 'at, love?'

' 'Ow do I know? It's not *in* me 'at.'

'Where's 'is 'at?'

Another voice said, 'He's sittin' on ut.'

'Stand up, love. Come on, I'll 'old yer. Tha's right. Now let's 'ave a dekko at yer 'at.'

'Hey! That's me good 'at. Who sat on ut? Hey, you! Did you sit on me 'at?'

'Yer sat on ut yerself.'

140

'Don' gimme that. Ut's me good 'at. Think I'd sit on me good 'at? Man oughta crown yer.'

'Don' worry about ut, love. Yer c'n get a new one Mondy. 'Ere's yer ticket.'

'Where was ut?'

'In yer 'at.'

'Couldna been. Put ut in with me 'alf a quid.'

'No, yer couldna put ut in with yer 'alf a quid, love, because ut was in yer 'at. Now you just lie down an' go ter sleep.'

'No. Don' like the blokes up 'ere. One of 'em sat on me 'at.'

'Well, you come down an' sleep with us, love. We'll find room for yer.'

'Me good 'at. Some bloke sat on me good 'at.'

The small man's voice was coming closer. 'Just lean on me shoulder, love. Yer won't fall over. Come on, ut's not far.'

I was interested to see this man called 'Love'. It was a strange name. He was enormous. His big hand covered the small man's shoulder.

'Hang on tight, now.' The small man kicked his sleeping companion's leg. 'Hey, wake up. Come on, wake up.'

The man woke up. 'Wassa matter? We there?'

'No, we ain't there. Got a long way ter go yet. Got company.'

'Gee, where'd yer find 'im?'

'Up the other end. Move over an' we'll put 'im in the middle. There y'are, love. You sit down between us. We'll look after yer.'

'Love' sat down. He left very little room for the other two. He sat completely upright. He had a broad, pleasant face which wore an expression of faint worry.

'Where's me 'at?' he said.

141

'On yer 'ead, love. Now go to sleep.'

An official came along calling 'Tickets, please.' The two men produced their tickets.

'Love' said, 'Ut's 'ere somewhere. Put ut in with me 'alf a quid.'

The official ignored him and turned to us. 'Tickets, please.'

He grasped Joe's shoulder and shook him. 'Tickets, please.' Joe sat up and pushed his hat back from his eyes.

'Wot? Aw, why d'you blokes always come round when a bloke's asleep? Pat. Dennis. Fork out yer tickets. The vulture's 'ere.'

Pat and Dennis woke grumbling. We surrendered our tickets.

'Where are we?' Pat asked.

'Dunno. Can't be far orf, but. 'Ave a look at the next stop. 'Owyagoin', Nino?'

'Orright, Joe.'

'That's the ticket.'

'Love' said, 'Ut's 'ere somewhere. Put ut in with me 'alf a quid.'

The small man said, 'Aw, change the record, will yer, love?'

'Bloke over there wants me ticket. Ut's 'ere somewhere.'

' 'E doesn't want yer ticket. The snapper's got yer ticket.'

'Bloke over there said 'e wanted me ticket.'

'No 'e didn't. Where's yer whisky?'

' 'Ow do I know? Ut's 'ere somewhere.'

'Yer musta left ut up the other end. I'll get ut.'

'Love' spread into the vacant space. He looked long and solemnly at me. He pointed at me. He said, 'Who's that bloke?'

The other man said, 'Dunno. 'E's not one of our mob.'

'Sat on me 'at,' 'Love' said. 'Sat on me good 'at.'

'No, 'e didn't.'

'Love' leaned across the aisle and put his giant hand on my knee. 'It was me good 'at. Wodyer sit on me good 'at for?'

The small man came back. 'Move over, love,' he said. 'Got yer whisky. Now we're all set.'

'Give us a swig,' said the other man. He drank from the bottle. The small man drank from the bottle. 'Want some, love?'

'No. Bloke over there sat on me good 'at.'

The small man held the bottle towards me. 'Care fer a swig, mate?'

'No, thank you,' I said.

'Wot about you blokes?'

'Never knock it back,' said Pat and Dennis together.

'Count me out, matey,' Joe said.

The train stopped. Dennis looked out the window. 'Helensburgh,' he said. 'Won' be long now.'

'Where yez goin'?' said the small man.

'Stanwell Park. Knock over a few rabbits.'

'Wondered wot yez was doin' with the guns. Finished with me bottle?'

'Yes, thanks. That was good.'

'Belongs ter me mate, but 'e's 'ad ut.'

'Shouldn' talk to 'em,' said 'Love'. 'Sat on me good 'at.'

When we reached Stanwell Park it was still dark. It was also raining. Dennis was disgusted.

'Wouldn' ut! Just our bloody luck!'

'Good huntin',' said the small man.

'Thanks. Be seein' yer.'

'Yeah. See yer.'

We got out. So did all the Boy Scouts.

'Gawd,' said Pat. 'Hope *they're* not goin' where we're goin'.'

Apparently they were. They were all around us as Joe led us down a slippery track. They were very small scouts. It was difficult to avoid treading on them.

'Gunna be a bastard tryin' to find a dry spot.'

'Hunt up a cow.'

'If we c'n find one.'

We crossed a bitumen road and climbed through a fence. The scouts went along the road.

'Thank the Lord fer that. Thought they were gunna swarm all over us.'

'Know where yer goin', Joe?'

'Course I know where I'm bloody goin'. Think a man's a dill?'

'Aw, yer not a dill *all* the time, I'll say that for yer.'

'Know a coupla trees. Just right fer slingin' the tent.'

'Be daylight soon.'

'Daylight now. Look at 'er gettin' light in the east.'

' 'Ow der yer know where's east?'

Dennis began to sing:

> 'Ship me somewheres east o' Suez
> Where the best is like the worst.'

'Not a bad song, that. If yer could sing. Sound like an old crow with 'is foot caught in a rabbit trap.'

Dennis stopped singing.

'Sing some more, Dennis. That is a good song.'

'No. Me feelin's are 'urt.'

Joe found his two trees. The tent was suspended on a rope tied to each tree. The side ropes were held down with stones. It was only a small tent, and it was very crowded when we all crawled into it. The ground was stony and wet. It was still raining softly. Our clothes were wet.

'Nice an' dry in 'ere,' Joe said.

I did not agree with him. I was cold and tired.

'Grab a bit o' shut eye. Dig out the groundsheets, Den.'

Dennis spread two thin rubber sheets on the ground.

'Wot about some brekker?' Pat said.

' 'Ave ut when we wake up, matey. Snore orf first.'

We lay on the thin rubber, on the small stones, on the wet ground, and I was surprised later to find that I had fallen asleep almost immediately. I woke to find Joe shaking me.

'Time ter shake a leg,' he said.

I sat up, and my body was stiff and sore. I would have liked to sit in a chair or lie on a bed.

'What is the time?' I said.

'Haven't a clue, matey. None o' these drongos brought their watches. Got yours?'

I had no watch. The rain had stopped, but the sky was heavily clouded.

'Might be afternoon,' Dennis said. 'Coulda slept all day.'

'Time fer a feed, anyway,' said Pat.

'Good idea, matey. Scrounge around an' see if yer c'n dig up some dry wood. You c'n go down the creek, Den, and fill the billy.'

'Wot're you gunna do?'

'I'll stay with Nino and dig out the tucker.'

'Don' bust yerself.'

Dennis and Pat went away, and Joe began spreading the contents of the pack on the groundsheets.

'Bread, butter, knife—glad they thought o' the knife; last time we went shootin' no bugger 'ad one—meat, salt, forks, coupla tins o' stew—that'll do us fer now. Heat up the stew

K

in the billy and then make the tea. Stew an' dodger. Suit yer, Nino?'

'Yes, Joe.'

'Good-o. Make a place fer the fire.'

He made a small circular enclosure with stones. Dennis came back with a can of water. Pat brought strips of bark and an armful of sticks.

'Dry?' said Joe.

'Dry enough.'

They started a fire. The smell of the burning bark and sticks was very pleasant. They removed the labels from the tins of stew, and put the tins in the can of water. When the water boiled they removed the tins and made tea. We ate the stew from tin plates, and washed it down with hot black tea.

'Beats all yer bloody spaghetti,' Pat said.

'Grilled steak fer tea.'

' 'Ow der yer know we're not 'avin' tea now? Can't see the sun. Could be afternoon.'

'Go over ter the shop later,' Joe said. 'Find out.'

The meal was refreshing. I felt much better. I looked at the country around us. We were on the side of a hill on which a few trees grew, together with hard brown grass. We could see the sea. Inland were forest-covered hills. At the bottom of the hill a stream flowed towards the sea. After our meal we crossed this stream, and Joe led us to a small shop near many tents. A woman was sweeping its floor. She came to the door as we approached.

'Gooday,' Joe said.

'Day.'

'Any idea o' the time?'

'Ut's early yet.'

'Oh.' To us he whispered, 'Can't ask 'er if ut's mornin' or

afternoon. She'll think we're a bunch o' dills.' Aloud he said, 'Wot time does that bus go?'

'In about 'arf an hour.'

'Oh. (Not gettin' anywhere, are we?) Wot time do yer close up?'

'Aw, when ut gets dark.'

We looked at her. She looked at us.

'Got any Minties?' Dennis said.

'Plenty.'

'Give us a zac's worth.'

We entered the shop.

'Don't be lousy,' said Pat. 'Buy a bob's worth.'

'Orright. Give us a bob's worth.'

She weighed the Minties.

'Got any matches?' Joe asked her.

'Yes. How many yer want?'

'One'll do. Got ours wet last night.'

'Yes, it rained a lot last night.'

'Rain much this mornin'?'

'Yes. Where were youse this mornin'?'

'Snorin' orf.'

'Where yez camped?'

'Up on the hill.'

'No one there yesterdy.'

'No. Come in on the paper train.'

'Lotta Boy Scouts come on that. Camped up the other side there.'

'Yeah. We saw 'em.'

They paid for the Minties and matches.

'Anything else yez want?'

'Got any torch batteries?' Pat asked. 'Mine's on the blink. Might be dark when we get back.'

'Wot size?'

Pat indicated the size with his hands.

'Yeah. I got some o' them. Where yez goin'?'

'Shootin',' Pat said. 'Up the hills.'

'Won't shoot nothin' up there. Some rabbits down the blackberries. Might get some of them if yer wait till sunset fer 'em ter come out. Yer c'n put in the day doin' somethin' else.'

'Nothin' up there, eh?'

'Nothin'.'

'Orright. Forget about the torch batteries. We'll 'ave a crack at the rabbits later before we go 'ome. Be seein' yer.'

'Ta-ta,' she said.

We left the shop.

'Go this way,' Dennis said. ' 'Ave a look at the surf.'

We walked along the beach. The sea was rough. I said, 'I did not understand all that conversation in the shop. Did you find out what is the time?'

'We're sweet,' Joe said. 'Still mornin'.'

'Where were all those men going, who were on the train?'

'Wollongong, probably.'

'That Mr. Love was the biggest man I've seen in Australia.'

'Who?'

'Mr. Love.'

They laughed. 'Not *Mr*. Love,' Joe said, 'just love. 'E was the little bloke's mate.'

'Oh. Then why was he called love instead of mate?'

'I dunno. Don' know much about coal miners.'

'If yer thinkin' 'e was a queer,' Pat said, 'I got a quid ter say 'e wasn't.'

'I got *five* quid,' said Dennis.

We climbed the hill to the tent.

'There is one other question I wish to ask, I said.

'Ask on, matey.'

'What sort of an animal is a lagoon?'

'A goon?'

'No. A lagoon.'

' 'Aven't a clue.'

'Wodda yer talkin' about?' Dennis said.

'At the end of the beach was a notice on which was written "Do Not Let the Lagoon Out".'

They stopped walking, and held on to each other, and laughed very much.

Joe finally said, 'Can't beat 'im, can yer? Good as a tonic, 'e is. Glad we brought 'im.'

'You have not answered my question, Joe. What is a lagoon?'

'Kind of a platypus,' Pat said.

'Yeah,' said Dennis. 'With radar instead of ears. Kook-kook-kook-kook-kook.'

I looked it up in my dictionary the next week, and understood their laughter.

At the tent they busied themselves wiping and oiling their rifles. Dennis put his over his shoulder and said, 'Be seein' yer.' He left the tent.

'Where is Dennis going, Joe?'

'Always goes orf on 'is own when we go shootin'. Moody bastard.'

Pat said, 'Up the creek, eh?'

'Yeah. Good a place as any.'

They finished playing with their rifles, and we went out and crossed the road, and went under a railway bridge, and along the banks of the stream into the hills. We climbed cliffs and steep slopes, and reached a flat rock on top of the range, from which there was a wonderful view of coast and ocean. We had seen nothing at which to shoot.

'Old dame was right,' Pat said. 'Nothin' up 'ere.'

'Yeah. Good place ter teach Nino ter shoot, but. Fix up a target, Pat.'

'Wot with?'

'Anything yer like.'

'Wot about yer 'ead?'

'No. Need ut ter nut out jobs fer you blokes. Use yer own if yer like.'

'Don't believe in cruelty to bullets.' He put a cigarette paper in the bark of a tree. ' 'Ow will that be?'

'Good enough. 'Ave a crack at ut, Nino.'

I hit it with my third shot.

'Fair enough. Now stick one further away an' give an expert a go.'

Pat put a cigarette paper in another tree. He came back as Joe was aiming at it.

'Hey! Wodda yer think *you're* doin'! There's only one expert around here.'

'Know that, matey. Stand aside.'

They fired many shots, and the target was destroyed. The clouds had thinned, and the sun was trying to shine.

'Good place ter snore orf,' Joe said.

We lay on the warm rock. Pat and Joe went to sleep. I looked at the sky and thought of Sundays in Italy—the church bells and the best clothes and the visiting and the enormous meals. I had not been to Mass. But God is close when a man is on a mountain, and I did not feel very guilty. My family was a long way away, and I was in the hands of these two Australians asleep on a rock. I felt that the hands were strong and kind. The nails were broken, and not very clean, but they were capable hands. With a rifle, a shovel, a mattock or a trowel. With a woman? Yes. Would an Italian wife permit her husband to leave her in the middle of the night as Joe had left his wife? On what were Australian marriages based? Sex? Friendship? Mutual dependence? This would be a subject for me to investigate for my writing. Were Joe and Edie typical of Australian marriage? I had much to learn. About courtship, too. Was Dennis' and Pat's attitude towards girls typical? Could Italians of their age spend a day happily without feminine company? Could I, if I were home? Girls with their chatter and their demands for attention would spoil the peace of this day, this rock, this quiet sky, these trees. Without them, a man in a city was a lonely nothing. Without them, a man on a mountain was content. Perhaps there was something to write about in this also. I would think about it. Thinking about it, I also went to sleep, and woke perspiring to find the clouds gone, the sun shining from a clear sky, and the rock uncomfortably hot. Joe and Pat were sitting in the shade with their backs to a tree. I sat up.

Joe said, 'Good on yer, Nino. Yer won me a dollar. I bet Pat yer'd wake up before the shade o' this tree hit yer.'

'Take ut outa me wages,' said Pat. 'Ready ter start down?'

'Yeah. Been up 'ere long enough. Come on, Nino. Back ter camp.'

'Dennis oughta be back by now,' Pat said. 'Bet y' another dollar 'e's got a rabbit.'

'Yer on, mate.'

We climbed down to the stream. A deep pool was tempting. We took off our clothes and got into it. It was cold and clean.

At the tent, Dennis was sitting under one of the trees watching a new fire licking at the billy.

'Wot's cookin'?' said Joe.

'Rabbit stew.'

'How many d'yer get?'

'Four.'

'Makes ten bob y' owe me, Pat.'

'No ut don't.'

'Why don't ut?'

'You bet me Dennis would get *a* rabbit. 'E got four rabbits. That's not *a* rabbit. We're all square.'

'Gees, you shoulda been a lawyer. Save the skins, Den?'

'Summer skins. Not worth savin'.'

'Ain't yer gunna ask us 'ow many *we* got?'

'No need ter. Y'ain't carryin' any.'

'How near is ut ter bein' cooked, matey?'

' 'Bout five minutes.'

'Good-o. We c'd go a bit o' that. Ever tasted rabbit stew before, Nino?'

'No, Joe.'

'Got a treat comin' ter yer, matey. She's an extra good brew.'

So 'she' was. There was none left when we'd finished.

'Wot now?' said Pat.

'Wash up, pack up an' go 'ome,' Joe said.

'Wot about all this tucker we got left? Take ut with us?'

'Give ut ter the dear little Boy Scouts,' said Dennis. 'We c'n go past 'em on the way up.'

We did this, and the Scout Master thanked us most profusely. The sun was low over the hills when we left him.

Dennis was curious. 'Wot makes a bloke become one o' those blokes? Mob o' kids like that'd drive yer mad.'

'Takes all sorts, matey,' Joe said. 'Probably gets a kick outa bossin' 'em around.'

'I'd wanta kick all their little arses.'

'Oo, you cruel man,' said Pat. 'Wot about tryin' fer a coupla rabbits in them blackberries? We got tons o' time.'

'Good-o, matey. 'Ave ter sneak up on 'em, but.'

We lay in the long grass and waited until the sun disappeared behind the hills, but no rabbits appeared.

'Give ut away,' Joe said. 'Get the next train.'

We were not alone going up the hill to the station. There were numerous young men and girls, carrying packs and baskets, and pushing and pummelling each other, shouting and laughing. Dennis disapproved.

'Dunno which is worse—the dear little Boy Scouts or this slap an' tickle mob.'

'Garn, yer was young yerself once.'

'Not that young.'

'One thing,' Joe said, 'plenty trains this time of a Sunday night. Won't 'ave ter wait long.'

'Lucky if we get a seat.'

There were no vacant seats. Every seat in the train that arrived half an hour later was occupied. We sat on the tent and pack in the corridor, crushed in a crowd of young people who flirted and giggled and sang songs all the way to Sydney. I enjoyed it very much. Dennis became more and more irritable.

'Next bugger treads on me foot I'll land 'im one,' he said in a loud voice to no particular person.

A red-haired young man in a white T-shirt said, 'Referrin' ter me?'

'Referrin' to anyone who treads on me foot.'

'Why don't yer shift yer foot?'

'Where the hell c'n I shift ut to? Why don't you sit down?'

'Where the hell c'n I sit down? Try landin' *me* one an' yer'll be sorry.'

'Tread on me foot. Go on, tread on me foot.'

I would have liked to have joined in the singing, but I did not know the songs.

'Do you know these songs, Dennis?' I asked him.

'Yeah. Tripe.'

'What would you like to sing?'

' 'Nough bloody row goin' on without us joinin' in.'

'Been thinkin',' Joe said. 'Where'd yer get them four rabbits, Den?'

'In the blackberries.'

'Mighta known ut.'

'Shot the bloody lot,' Pat said. 'Probably only four there. Us 'angin' around waitin', an' 'im sayin' nothin'. Know wot you are, Den? Yer a bastard.'

'Yeah. I'm a real drip.'

'You said ut,' the young man in the T-shirt said.

Dennis started to get up. 'I've 'ad you,' he said. 'I'm gunna drop yer.'

Joe and Pat pulled him down again.

'Know who this bloke is?' Joe asked.

T-shirt didn't know.

'Go ter the Stadium next week and yer'll see 'im fightin' Freddie Dawson.'

'Cripes,' T-shirt said. 'Sorry, mate.'

'That's orright. Just thought I'd warn yer. I'm 'is trainer.'

' 'Ow der yer reckon 'e'll go?'

'Yer c'n put a quid on 'im.'

Dennis unexpectedly grinned at Joe. 'Sometimes I wonder why I work fer you,' he said, 'an' sometimes I know.'

'Woulda been murder, matey. 'E's only about eighteen.'

'So ut costs 'im a quid instead.'

'Yeah. Cheap at 'alf the price.'

'Yer a bastard, Joe.'

'That's wot Edie reckons. Gunna be trouble when we get 'ome. She put up 'ardly any fight when we come away last night. That bit of a chip on 'er shoulder'll be a ten inch log be now.'

154

'Yer c'n always sleep at our place.'

'Might 'ave ter, matey.'

But Edie greeted us very pleasantly when we reached Joe's house. She made coffee and toast for us all. She said she was worried about us when it started raining. And how many rabbits did we get?

'On'y four, love. Dennis got 'em. Don' know how he did ut, but. They don't come outa those blackberries until sundown.'

'Cloudy,' Dennis said. 'Knew they'd be out.'

'And did *you* have a good day, Nino?'

'I had a very good day, thank you, Edie.'

'Well, I think you should all have a hot shower now, and go to bed. You've got a big day to-morrow. Don't be too long, Joe. I'll stay awake till you come in.' She went into their bedroom.

'Don' like the sound o' that,' Joe said. 'Round o' the kitchen comin' up. Better put cotton wool in yer ears, Nino.'

'Leave yer to ut,' said Dennis. 'Grab some shut-eye. Yell if yer want help.'

'She'll be sweet, matey. Nothin' I can't handle.'

'Famous last words. See yer ter-morrer if yer still in one piece.'

He and Pat went home.

'You c'n 'ave first go at the shower, Nino. I'll 'ang around fer a while an' do a bit o' work on them plans. Man never knows 'is luck. She might go ter sleep.'

Chapter Eleven

You have seen that my first few days amongst Australians gave me a very good introduction to these unusual people, and to their strange language. I do not wish it to be thought that I remembered every word that was said. I remembered much of it, but the rest has come from later knowledge, which gives me the words that must have been used at the time. The people I have been talking about have been my friends for years now, and they still talk and behave in the same way. So do I. Good English, used in conversation, now appears stilted and insincere. My Australian friends say that a man who uses it is not fair dinkum. They say he 'is bungin' ut on'. It is not so much the choice of words that is offensive to the Australian's ear, but the pronunciation and inflexion. For instance, I have a friend named Addo who uses words well and any advanced student of English would understand him perfectly. But the student would know, from his accent and inflexion, that Addo was not an Englishman. And the conversation of most of my other friends would be completely unintelligible to him, as it was to me for so long. It was both irritating and humbling to me to have all my remarks clearly understood, and to be myself unable to understand the replies. And when I did get the hang of the lingo, to be unable to use it in my Italian articles was infuriating. Those first few days gave me sufficient material to keep my articles going for a long time, but I was completely unable to enliven their dialogue. Now I have put it down as it was and is, and I am more contented with myself.

I wish I could reproduce the accent, and the close lipped rapid enunciation. I have thought of using a tape recorder to capture it. But when an Australian is asked to speak for a specific purpose, everything that makes his conversations the delight they are, disappears. For a man who is such an extrovert in his daily life with his mates, his shy embarrassment before a microphone or an audience, is unbelievable. Even when sitting with his mates at lunchtime, amongst the sandwich wrappings and tea leaves, his embarrassment when asked to tell a story, is very real. He becomes almost inarticulate. His whole speech changes, his phrasing becomes stilted. He rushes through the story to its end, gives a self-deprecating smile, and goes back to conversation happily on politics, horses, cars, football, beer, the boss without any self-consciousness at all. It is very strange. I have heard him make long and impassioned speeches to his friends in argument. Asked to repeat his sentiments before an attentive audience, he can say nothing. His personality withers immediately.... Ask him to read a newspaper article aloud, and he adopts a monotonous sing song voice that kills the subject matter dead. Say to him, 'Never mind readin' the bloody thing, give us the guts of ut ... wot does ut say?' and he'll tell you, in vivid phrases whose economy of words, and whose pungent analysis are masterpieces. If you can understand them.

So, you New Australians who think you can speak English, do not be discouraged. Keep listening, and you'll catch on in time. And if you are ever admitted to an Australian's friendship, thank your God for one of the finest things that can happen to you in this life. He will talk to anybody and everybody, this Australian, but his real mates are few. For them, he will die. Literally.

I do not think I will take a tape recorder and try to capture his natural conversations without his knowledge. He might find out, and for this I would probably die. I am not at all sure I will live long, anyway, if this book is ever published.

There is one other piece of information and advice I will give you. The Australian will endure an incredible amount of abuse from his friends, and none at all from anybody else. So don't call him a bastard just because you hear somebody else do so.

You will notice that I have said very little about Australian women. This is because I know very little about Australian women. I have observed that they appear to be independent, and do not sublimate their lives to that of some man, as most of our Italian women do. They keep their friendship for those of their own sex, and appear to be more or less constantly at war with men. The marriages I have observed seem more like armed truces than partnerships. This statement will probably endanger my life, too, but I have not observed many marriages. My own is different. I would be very foolish to say otherwise. But I will justify my father's confidence in my courage by braving the flying pots and pans to tell you something about it. I like to think that I chose my wife in my own way and in my own time. She assures me this is not so. But one thing is certain. When I met her, I was hunting for a wife.

I had been in Australia more than two years. I no longer wrote articles for Italian magazines, but Joe had taught me well, and I was earning good money, as a bricklayer. I had applied for naturalization as an Australian. I had money in the bank. I still lived with Joe and Edie. It was my third winter here. It was Sunday afternoon, and raining. And it was cold. Joe and Edie were sitting by the fire. Edie was knitting, and Joe had his feet upon the brickwork of the fireplace. He was reading the Sunday papers. The cat was asleep between them. I was restless. I walked in and out of the room several times.

Edie said, 'Nino, for goodness sake sit down. You're making me drop stitches.'

I sat down, and I made a decision. 'Joe,' I said. 'I am going to get married.'

'Good on yer, mate.' he said, and went on reading.

Edie was more interested. 'Nino,' she said. 'I had no idea. Who is it?'

'Dark horse, the old Nino,' said Joe.

I said, 'It is no one yet. I have just decided.'

'Oh,' she said, disappointed. 'I thought you meant soon.'

'It will be soon. I am going to look for a girl, and I am going to marry her.'

Edie looked thoughtful.

Joe said, 'Now don't go thinkin' up any o' your scrawny mates. Where'll yer look, Nino?'

'I do not know yet,' I said.

Joe said to Edie, 'Where der the sheilas go these days when they're on the prowl?'

'How would I know?'

'Well if you wouldn't, who would?'

'I don't know,' she said.

'Ask Dennis an' Pat, matey. They know all the lurks.' He returned to his papers.

I went next door. Dennis and Pat were playing darts on the back verandah.

'Want a game?' Pat said.

'No, thank you Pat,' I said. 'I want to find a sheila.'

'Wot sheila?'

'Any sheila. I want to get married.'

Dennis said, 'Gees yer don't just marry any sheila.'

'Yer wanter shop around,' said Pat.

'Where is a good place to shop around?' I said.

Dennis sat down and began to roll a cigarette. 'A knotty problem. A very knotty problem. Wodda yer reckon Pat?'

'Yeah, a knotty problem.' He sat down and began to roll a cigarette also. 'Wot sorta sheila yer have in mind?'

'No particular sort.'

'Blondes are easy on the eye,' Dennis said. 'But they get dirty quick.'

'Redheads are too quick on the trigger,' Pat said. 'Bite yer 'ead orf. Remember that one I 'ad last year in Sans Souci?'

'Gees yes,' said Dennis. 'Better make ut a brunette. They're nice an' faithful.'

'Generally got hairy legs, but,' Pat said.

'Yer can't 'ave everything. Most of 'em are put together right.'

'Yeah. I'll say that for 'em.'

'Wot about . . .? No. She wouldn't do.'

'Know who yer mean. Agree with yer.'

'Got any clues?'

'Not a clue.'

'When der yer wanter get married?'

'As soon as possible.'

'Wet Sundy,' said Pat.

'Yeah. See wot yer mean,' said Dennis.

They sat and smoked thoughtfully. I waited.

'Wot about Bondi?' said Pat.

'Too wet.'

'Manly?'

'The Corso. Could be yeah. 'Bout the best bet.'

'Want us ter come with yer?'

'Thank you, but I would rather go alone.'

'Probably safer. Line up somethin' good an' she's likely ter latch onter me or Pat.'

I said, 'Manly, do you think?'

'Yeah. Manly, we think. Goin' now?'

'I think I will go now. Yes.'

'Good huntin'.'

They went back to the game. As I left I heard Pat say, 'Reckon he's fair dinkum?'

'No,' Dennis said. 'Weather's got 'im.'

It was very late in the afternoon when I reached Manly. I had been there before. The wind and the rain made the ferry trip unpleasant. The Corso was practically deserted. Between the ferry and the beach I saw only one interesting looking girl. I smiled at her. A freckled face with most of its front teeth missing, who was walking behind her, smiled back. I walked up the other side, and back to the ferry.

Then I started again. This time I did not see one interesting looking girl. And I began to feel hungry. Also I was wet and cold. I went into a café near the beach, and sat down. There were only a few people there. Two of them were girls sitting together. They were working out a crossword puzzle. The Saturday *Herald* one, which is very difficult. This showed that they were intelligent, and I observed them more closely. One had fair skin and light brown hair, and the other had olive skin and was a brunette. I liked the one with the brown hair. She noticed that I was watching her and said something to the brunette. This one looked directly at me in a most severe manner. She did not appear to approve of my interest in her friend.

The waiter brought them bowls of spaghetti, and then

L

came to my table. I ordered spaghetti also. The two girls removed their *Herald*, and began to eat their spaghetti. They used a spoon. They had much difficulty. The fair one was laughing over this difficulty, but the brunette appeared to me to be swearing. She seemed to be a very bad tempered girl. I thought I would help them, so I got up and went to their table.

I said, 'Excuse me, but it is not possible to eat spaghetti with a spoon.'

The brunette said, 'Mind your own business.'

The fair one smiled and said, 'How do you eat the damn stuff?'

'With a fork,' I said. 'You hold the fork upright, and twirl it around. The spaghetti winds itself on. Then you eat it.'

The waiter passed, going to my table.

The fair one said, 'Are you having spaghetti?'

'Yes, I am.'

'Well, bring it over here, an' show us how.'

This I did. I sat down opposite to them. The fair one soon managed very well. The brunette continued to use the spoon.

I said to her, 'Please try it with the fork. It's much easier.'

She said again, 'Mind your own business.'

I said, 'I am trying to help you. I will introduce myself. I am Nino Culotta.'

She said, 'I won't tell anybody.'

She appeared to be very irritable and really was swearing at this spaghetti. But she continued trying to make it stay on the spoon.

The fair one said, 'They call me Dixie, this is Kay.'

I said, 'How do you do Dixie? How do you do Kay?'

They did not answer.

Dixie said, 'What are you doing out on an evening like this?'

'I am looking for a wife.'

'Whose?'

'Nobody's. I mean, I wish to get married, and I am looking for someone who is my type, and whom I can marry.'

The brunette looked up at me. She had large blue eyes. They were very cold. She said, 'Have you tried the Zoo?'

I said, 'You do not appear to like me very much.'

'Give me three reasons why I should.'

'I am strong. I am not married. I have money in the bank.'

'Think up three other reasons,' she said, and took up her spoon again.

Dixie said, 'That last reason's very interesting. How much?'

'Are you interested in getting married?'

'Maybe.'

Kay said, 'Charlie'll be here soon.'

'Yeah,' said Dixie. 'Charlie!'

I said, 'Who is Charlie?'

'The man I'm going to marry.'

'Oh,' I said. 'You are engaged?'

'Sort of.'

'What does that mean?'

'Oh, I s'pose I'll marry him someday.'

'You'd better,' Kay said. 'He'll break your neck if you don't.'

'Yeah. He might too.'

'Are you engaged?' I asked Kay.

Dixie said, 'No she's free . . . at the moment.'

Kay kicked her under the table. Dixie said, 'Ouch. What was that for?'

'I think you are a very bad tempered young lady,' I said.

163

'And I think you ought to mind your own business.'

'Now children!' Dixie said. 'No fighting in public.'

'You are bad tempered, but you have very beautiful eyes.'

'Thanks.'

'And I like your hair. It is very clean.'

She looked at me for a long moment. Then she put her leg out to the side of the table.

'What do you think of my foot?' she said.

I looked at it. 'It appears to be a very nice foot. You should not kick people with it.'

'I know somebody I'm going to kick very soon.'

Dixie said, 'What did you say your name was?'

'Nino Culotta.'

'Italian?'

'Yes. But I will be an Australian soon.'

'Alas my country,' Kay said.

'Are you always so serious Nino?' Dixie said. 'Or are you just having us on?'

'Courting is a serious matter.'

'I thought that word died with Queen Victoria,' Kay said.

Dixie became coy. 'Are you courting, Nino?'

'Yes.'

'Little me?'

'No,' I said. 'You are engaged. I am courting Kay.'

'Great suffering cats,' said Kay. 'What have I done to deserve this?'

'Perhaps courting is not the correct word,' I said. 'I am still learning English as it is spoken in Australia. But I think it is time for me to get married. To do this, I must meet girls, and talk with them, and maybe I will find one whom I like, and who likes me, and then perhaps we will get married. I call this process courting. Is there a better word?'

'Yeah,' said Dixie. 'I know one.'

'Shut up,' said Kay. She looked at me, and I saw a little interest in her eyes. She said, 'Are you serious?'

'Yes,' I said. 'I am very serious.'

'Seems a cold blooded way to go about it.'

'What's wrong with the girls in Italy?' Dixie asked me.

'There are some very nice girls in Italy. But I am not there. I am in Australia.'

'Yeah. Makes a difference, I s'pose. How many have you tried out so far?'

'None. You two are the first.'

'And you drew a blank with me, because of Charlie, drat him.'

'Do you ever smile?' Kay said.

'Yes.'

She leaned across the table. 'Well, smile.'

I did so.

'Good teeth,' she said. 'Let's have a look at your finger-nails.'

I showed her my hands.

'H'm. Reasonably clean. How often do you shave?'

'Every morning.'

'Your hair needs cutting.'

'Yes, I know. I have not had time.'

'You should make time. It is most important. What size shoes do you wear?'

'Size eight.'

'Any corns?'

'No.'

'Bunions?'

'No.'

'Varicose veins?'

'What are they?'

'You'd know, if you had them. No varicose veins. Have you ever had any serious illness?'

'I had measles when I was a child.'

'Perhaps we can overlook that. Any insanity in your family?'

'No.'

'I don't agree with you, but we'll skip that. Were your father and mother married?'

'Yes.'

'And you are not married?'

'No.' I laughed.

'All this, and it laughs too.' There was amusement in her eyes. 'Okay, when do we start?'

'When do we start what?'

'Courting.'

Dixie's voice broke in excitedly. 'Kay. You're not serious?'

'Why not. He gets to know me, I get to know him. At the moment I think he's a nuisance, and he thinks I'm bad tempered. We could both be right, or we could both be wrong. I think I'll find out.'

'But . . . Golly! Gee! I never thought . . . Charlie! Charlie, come here.'

A man was entering. He said, 'I'm coming there. Wot's up?'

He came to the table.

Dixie said, 'Charlie, this is Nino.'

I said, 'How do you do?' and he said, 'Hi-yah.'

'Charlie they're courting.'

'They're what?'

'Courting.'

'Who is?'

'Kay and Nino.'

'No,' said Charlie. 'Gee c'n anybody watch?'

He pulled up a chair to the head of the table. He put his elbows on the table. So did Dixie. They both watched me.

Dixie said, 'Well go on. Start.'

I was embarrassed. I said, 'I have already started.'

'Well, keep going.'

'The introduction is the start. This has been accomplished. It is not possible to do any more in public.'

'Men,' said Dixie. 'Just like you Charlie. He likes the dark.'

'Don't blame yer mate,' said Charlie. 'Where did yer dig him up, Kay?'

'He dug her up,' said Dixie.

'No,' Kay said. 'He wanted to be interested in Dixie. I took over.'

'Oh did he?' said Charlie. 'You could earn yourself a clout on the skull that way, mate.'

'I did not know she was engaged,' I said.

'No excuse. She's wearin' my brand.'

'Her left hand was under the table.'

He looked at her. His face was stern. 'Wot game are you playin'?' he said.

'Don't be silly. Can I help it if I'm attractive and fascinating to men?'

'Yes.'

'The game I like best,' I said, 'is soccer.'

Kay laughed. It seemed to change her personality. It made her look very attractive.

I said, 'You should laugh more often. It makes you look very attractive.'

'Oh, oh,' said Dixie. 'It's on.'

'She looks like a horse when she laughs,' Charlie said.

'That is not true. She looks very attractive.'

'All right, champ,' Kay said. 'The damsel is not in distress. How long have you been in Australia?'

'Quiz session,' said Dixie, 'coming up.'

'Keep quiet. I'm only being polite.'

'Polite. You were biting his head off a while ago.'

'That was a while ago. How long have you been in Australia, Nino?'

'Longer than two years.'

'And where do you live?'

'I live at Punchbowl.'

'Punchbowl! What's wrong with Alice Springs?'

'I do not know. I have not been there.'

'Soccer,' said Charlie, 'is a lousy game. Only dills play soccer.'

'Quiet, Charlie,' she said. 'Do you always take everything literally?' she asked me.

'He's a very literary fellow,' Dixie said.

'When I first came to Australia, I was. I was working for an Italian publishing house in Milano. I wrote many articles about Australia and Australians.'

'Highbrow,' said Dixie. 'That's why he needs a haircut.'

'Italians are dills,' Charlie said. 'They play soccer.'

'Your hands are not the hands of a writer,' Kay said.

'I do not write now,' I told her. 'Now I am a bricklayer.'

'Holy smoke,' said Dixie. 'Wouldn't he be popular at your place Kay? Kay's old man's a builder. He reckons he has to pay brickies twice as much as they're worth. He reckons all writers are parasites. And he can't stand Italians.'

'Can't blame him for that,' Charlie said. 'Place is gettin' lousy with 'em.'

'It is only getting lousy with Meridionali,' I told him. 'And I don't care whether Kay's old man likes Italians or not. And I'm rapidly approaching the stage where I've had you. So pull your scone in while it's still stuck to your neck.'

Kay applauded, 'Wow!' she said. 'Beware! This animal bites.'

'Are you lookin' for a thick ear?' Charlie said.

'You wouldn't last two minutes,' I told him. 'You'd find yourself lying out there in the gutter, and they'd have to get the council to come and shift you. Besides, it is not gentlemanly to fight in front of ladies.'

Charlie wanted to know, 'Wot ladies?'

'He's just cranky 'cause he hasn't had his tea,' Dixie said.

'I have had me tea. Went home an' changed before I come out.'

'Well you et too much.'

'Cold lamb an' lettuce an' tomatoes. How could y'eat too much o' that, this weather?'

'I dunno. But you did.'

'Was you there?'

'No. But I know you.'

'They're going to have a wonderful life together,' Kay said.

'Never a dull moment.'

'You keep out o' this,' Charlie told her.

Kay got up. 'We'll leave you to your happy little reunion,' she said. 'Would you like to escort me through the wilds of Manly, Nino?'

'Yes. I would like that very much.'

I helped her to put her raincoat on. She smiled and thanked me.

She said, 'See you to-morrow Dixie, if you're still in one piece.'

'Charlie's the one who'll be in pieces,' Dixie said.

I said, 'Goodnight Dixie. And thank you very much.

Goodnight Charlie. See you at a soccer match, sometime.'

Charlie grunted. We went out into the cold street. It was still raining.

Kay was laughing. She said, 'I think you're more than a match for Charlie boy.'

'I am sorry I became irritable.'

'You had a right to be. Charlie's all right, but he's terribly jealous. And for no reason, Dixie's just full of life.'

'She appears to be a very quick witted girl.'

'We work together. I like her.'

'So do I.'

'Yes I noticed that. We go this way.'

She took my arm. I liked that very much. I looked down at her. I said, 'Why were you so bad tempered when I came to your table?'

'Sorry about that. I thought you were just another wolf. I'm sick of them.'

'I am a wolf.'

She laughed. 'We go around here,' she said. 'What a night.'

'We are going to your home? You want me to meet your terrible father?'

'Not to-night . . . you're taking me as far as the church. I'm going to Benediction.'

'I hoped you would be a Catholic,' I said. 'I am one also. I will go with you.'

She stopped. We stood in the rain and the cold wind, and she said, 'Nino . . . Don't count on anything. I'm just . . . getting over some trouble. You call it a broken romance. I'd be scared to start another one.'

'I will not count on anything. We will go to the Benediction.' We continued walking.

'I love Benediction,' she said. 'It's so theatrical. The lights and the incense. It's beautiful.'

Inside the church it was bright and warm and dry. There were not many people there. I felt protective, kneeling alongside this small dark girl in her wet raincoat. I said some prayers for her.

and the person his friend is doing an advert... The John
and the person his friend is doing an advert... The John
I asked that in fact I was here apply warm and cast. There
were that many people at the party they were running on
a small bag, soft, dark and at the time, the waiters, it all
...

Chapter Twelve

WE went to the picture shows, and soccer matches, and
Rugby League. My workmates gave me a bad time.
They were very ribald and sarcastic and wanted to know
why I didn't let them meet her. If we decided to get married,
I told them, they would meet her. They said I was afraid they
would take her away from me. I said I was afraid she would
dislike me when she met the lousy company I kept. They
threw mortar at me. I threw mortar at them. We wasted an
hour cleaning down splashed brickwork. They became
hilarious when I bought a block of land. They designed a
house for me. It only had two rooms. One was a bedroom
and the other was a storeroom full of tinned foods. There
were barrels of beer above the bedroom ceiling, with rubber
tubes from them to the bed. There was a hole in the floor
leading to a chute which passed through the lower wall.
This was labelled, 'Kids. Keep well oiled.' At the chute's
outlet, a number of nurses were standing waiting with
baskets. These were labelled, 'Dago baskets'. They asked
me to submit the plan to Kay for her approval. I pretended
to have done so, and told them she was disappointed with it.
This was because there was no rhubarb, and she was very
fond of rhubarb. They modified the plan by putting a
rhubarb garden on the roof.

But they all came with me to inspect my land, and
approved of it. There was bushland at the back of the block,

and Dennis said there would be possums. This proved to be true. They offered to help me clear the block at week-ends. I said we could not do this until I knew definitely when I was getting married, because I would be busy courting at week-ends. They thought this was very funny.

'Jokin' aside,' Joe said. 'Reckon you'll marry this dame?'

'I think so,' I said. 'If she will have me.'

'When will yer know?'

'Soon. I cannot hurry matters. She is very shy.'

'Picked her up in a café, didn' yer?'

'Yes.'

'Can't be very shy.'

'She is shy of getting married. She was going to be married last year, but the man went away.'

'Strewth!' said Dennis. 'Wot's wrong with 'er?'

'There is nothing wrong with her. She is very attractive.'

They discussed what could be wrong with her, in a very rude manner. They decided that she squinted, was knock-kneed and had B.O. I denied this, vigorously. 'Only kiddin' yer matey,' Joe said. 'Edie wants ter meet 'er.'

'Don't everybody?' said Dennis.

Pat said he didn't. He was finished with women. This statement provoked much unbelieving laughter.

He said, 'I mean ut this time. I've had 'em.'

'They tell me knittin's a good substitute,' Joe said.

'Got a good'n lined up fer yer fer Saturdy night,' Dennis said.

'Couldn't care less, mate. I've had 'em. Had 'em all.'

'Wot's wrong with 'im?' Joe wanted to know.

'He got wiped last night. Wiped like a dirty rag.'

'Yeah. Yer haven't shaved she said. Yer fingernails are dirty, she said. Yer smell of beer, she said. I've had 'em.'

'These things are important,' I said. 'You should always shave and clean your fingernails before meeting a lady.'

'Listen ter the bloody expert, will yer? An' wot about the beer? Mean ter say a man's gotta go orf the grog before 'e meets 'em? Anyway, she wasn't a lady.'

'I'll give yer that,' Dennis said. 'She only thought she was. This other one's different.'

''Ave I gotta shave an' clean me fingernails?'

'Bloody oath yer have.'

'Nothin' doin'.'

'I'm tellin' yer she's worth ut.'

'Wot about beer?'

'Yer c'n 'ave a coupla middies.'

'A coupla middies? Yer know wot yer c'n do.'

'Yeah. An' I know wot you c'n do too. 'Ave a shave an' clean yer fingernails.'

'Where are we meetin' 'em?'

'Town Hall corner.'

'I'll turn up as full as an egg.'

'Good-o. Then I'll latch onto 'er meself.'

'I'll 'ave a look at 'er from the other side the road first.'

'Fair enough. Why don't you an' your sheila join us, Nino?'

'Have you not a girl Dennis?'

'Yes, I have not. But I'll have one by Saturdy. Got one lined up. Ringin' 'er ter-morrer.'

'Anyone we know?' Joe said.

'Wouldn' touch any you know with a forty foot pole.'

'Wot say me an' Edie join yez, an' we'll make ut a night?'

'Married men are barred.'

'No 'arm in tryin',' said Joe. 'Just wanted to 'ave a dekko at Nino's find.'

'All in good time, Joe,' I told him. 'No Dennis, I do not think we will join you on Saturday night.'

'Why? Reckon we've got leprosy?'

'You know it's not that. I wish to have a private conversation with Kay. I am to meet her parents on Sunday.'

'She's takin' yer ter meet the old folks? Yer gone a million, mate.'

'Before we make a decision, it is necessary for me to meet her family.'

'Nuttin' ut all out, ain't yer? Yer a cold blooded bastard.'

'I have already been told that, but I do not agree. I am just being sensible.'

'No. Cold blooded. Yer workin' ut all out as though yer was buyin' a truck. Lookin' 'em over in the second-hand joint: takin' 'em out for a trial run; checkin' on previous owners. Yer don't treat sheilas that way.'

'Has she got any cracks in the chassis?' Pat asked.

'Bet she needs new rings, anyway.'

'Usin' much oil?'

' 'Ow many miles ter the gallon does she do?'

'Seems to be a slow starter in cold weather.'

'Yeah, an' probably boils in the summer.'

'Wot about 'er front suspension?'

'An' 'er bumper bars?'

'Wot you need's a good mechanic ter look 'er over, Nino. Me and Dennis fer instance. We've 'ad lots of experience. We'll take 'er out on the road for yer, an' give y'an expert opinion.'

'Yeah, we'll vet 'er fer yer. Week-end after next eh?'

'I'll do the vettin',' said Joe. 'Owned one fer years. Know just wot makes 'em tick.'

'You've only 'ad experience with one model. That's no good.'

'All got the same sort o' engines, ain't they?'

'Different body work, but.'

'If we decide to get married you will meet her,' I told them.

'Wot if yer decide not ter get married?'

'Then I will have to look for somebody else. But I think we will marry.'

'Yeah,' said Joe thoughtfully. 'I think yer will. Yer showin' all the signs.'

'Fair dinkum, Nino,' Dennis said, 'is she orright?'

'Yes, Dennis. She is all right.'

'Ut's 'ard ter tell,' Pat said. 'They c'n fool yer.'

'Yer guarantee yer won't get married before we meet 'er?'

'Of course.'

'That's orright well. If she's not orright we'll know.'

'Yeah. We'll know.'

'No chiseller's goin' ter get 'er 'ooks inter 'im. Right?'

'Right.'

These were my friends. They would kid me, and abuse me, but they would see that no chiseller got her hooks into me. I was touched by their concern, and their loyalty. But I knew that it would embarrass them if I said so. So I said, 'You mob keep out of it. I can look after my bloody self.'

'Famous last words,' said Dennis.

'Textures,' said Joe.

'Wot are you mumblin' about?'

'Textures. They'll be the shot 'ere.'

'Textures? Against all those trees? Yer mad. Face bricks an' oiled timber.'

'Wattle bark an' a tin roof,' Pat said.

'No timber matey. Too much danger o' fire.'

'Not if yer clear all the big stuff orf 'er. She's a big block.'

'Get a fire in the top o' them trees and she'll go.'

176

'Get a fire in the top o' them trees, and a brick house'll go.'

'Better make 'er all fibro,' said Pat.

'No matey. Not fibro. No matter 'ow you do ut, fibro looks like a shack.'

'Not if yer paint ut.'

'Anyway fibro's too much work.'

'Yeah. There's a lot of work in ut.'

'I will build in brick and timber,' I said, 'and I will have face bricks inside, up to the window sills. And I will have vertical timber panelling above that. And I will put my ceiling above the rafters and I will dress and paint my rafters.'

They thought about this.

'Cost y'a packet,' Joe said.

'I will build it myself at week-ends,' I said.

'Gees matey, ut'll take y'a year or more.'

'Yes, but I will bring water and electricity to the block, and we will live in a tent while I am building.'

'If she falls fer that, she's no chiseller,' Dennis said.

Joe said, 'One o' the timber yards'll be glad ter take these trees. Yer'll 'ave ter grub the stumps out, but.'

We were sitting on the grass, amongst these trees. I could see in my mind my house being built. I could see it standing amongst lawns and shrubs, and flowers, with the bush behind it. I wanted to start. I wanted to get married. Joe put his hand on my shoulder, and stood up. 'Hope she doesn't turn yer down matey,' he said.

I was remembering his words all the week. I did not want her to turn me down. I was sure now that I wanted her for my wife. I wanted her for my wife, very much. But perhaps she would not want me. What had I to offer? I was a foreigner. No one of my blood was in this country. I was alone. I was proposing to ask her to marry a foreign bricklayer with no family. To live in a tent in the bush, whilst I cleared land and built a house. There would be metal and sand and brick-dust and sawdust and cement and mess everywhere. What would her parents say to this? If she agreed, they would say she was mad. And she would be mad. She could not possibly agree to it. I was mad. I was calmly proposing to ask this of a girl whom I had known only for a few weeks. I was certainly mad. So sure of myself that I had even bought the land. And planned the house. I was frightened. I could not believe that she would agree, and yet I hoped she would. I could not sleep. I worked and I worried. I walked and I prayed. When Saturday came I felt incapable of fighting even three Meridionali. I was no longer a man. I was inadequate. I was useless. I was a conceited fool.

I stepped off the ferry at Manly and saw Kay waiting for me. She was wearing a black suit, with an emerald green scarf at the throat, and not a hat. She looked beautiful and dignified, and unapproachable. I wanted to get back on the ferry. I wanted to go home. To Italy. To my mother and my father and my sisters and my brothers. Where I would not be lonely and useless and foolish and foreign. Where it would not matter what I was, because I was of their blood and therefore theirs, and I would always be welcome there. I knew I would be welcome there at this moment. Now. When I was walking so slowly towards God's finest creation, whom I had dared to think could be my wife. Nino Culotta's wife. Nino Culotta who wasn't worthy to touch even her gloved fingertips. Nino Culotta who wished he was home with his mother. But it was too late. She had seen him. Should he jump into the water? It would be wet and cold, and under the wharf it would be dark and he could hide amongst the piles. But his feet kept moving slowly forward, and she was approaching. Too quickly. She was moving towards him. Her shoes were bringing her. He looked at her shoes. Only at her shoes. They stopped in front of him. Her gloved hand touched his arm. He heard her voice. There was concern in it.

'Nino, what's the matter? Are you sick, Nino?'

'I am useless and foolish and conceited. You could not possibly marry a foreign bricklayer who has no family and only a tent to live in.'

The other gloved hand was under my chin, and pressing it up. 'Look at me,' she said.

I looked. She smiled. 'Poor Nino. Was it a bad week?'

'Yes. It was bad.'

'Nino, are you proposing to me? Here, amongst all these people?'

'I am very foolish. I wish to go home.'

'It was a bad week for me, too, Nino. I was afraid. I was afraid you wouldn't like me enough. And I wanted you to like me enough. Do you like me enough, Nino?'

I looked at her, and could not answer. But I must have answered without words.

She said softly, 'You and I are good for each other, Nino. I will be with you whenever you want me. And always, if you will let me.'

I could not speak. I could feel tears in my eyes.

She put her hand under my arm. 'Let's walk,' she said.

We walked all the way to the beach, and neither of us said anything. We looked at the waves breaking in the cool sunshine. I found my lost voice again. I said, 'Kay, did you mean what you said? You will marry me?'

'You know I will,' she said. 'No more tears?'

'I am sorry about that.'

'I'm not. I'm glad I saw them. And I'm glad you didn't

see mine last night. What was that about living in a tent?'

I told her my plan.

She said, 'Dad won't like that. But I will. You can show me what to do, and I'll help.'

I said, 'Kay, there is something else you should know.'

She looked worried. 'What?'

'I'm hungry.'

Her laughter was bright as the sun and the sea. I laughed with her. We ate steak and eggs at the café where we first met.

Italy was a terrible place. Who would want to go back there? My parents would probably be horrified if I arrived home to stay. They liked to think of their brave son amongst the savage Australians. All their friends would be reading his letters. I would send them a picture of Kay. Perhaps one day I would take her home for a holiday.

She interrupted my thoughts by saying, 'To-morrow night you will be having tea with my family. Scared?'

'Not now. Do I ask your father for his daughter's hand?'

'Good grief no. He'd die of shock. I'll tell him about it in the morning.'

'He will not die of shock then?'

'I think he knows. At least I think he's been hoping.'

'He need not worry. I will take care of you, Kay.'

'I know. I'm a very lucky girl.'

'How much costs an engagement ring?'

She laughed so much that she could not eat. The Australian sense of humour is sometimes very difficult to understand. I still have trouble with it at times.

When I told Joe and Edie on Sunday morning, Edie was very excited. Joe just said, 'Knew ut all along, mate.' But he went next door and told Pat and Dennis. They came in to congratulate me. They brought two bottles of beer with them.

Joe said, 'Wot time did you get up this mornin', Nino?'

'About half-past five.'

'Went to Communion, eh?'

'Yes.'

'Yer got ut bad, mate.'

Dennis said, 'When do we meet this paragon of feminine pulchritude?'

Pat said, 'Der woids. Cop der woids.'

Edie said, 'Bring her out next Sunday, Nino.'

'Yes, thank you, Edie. I will do that. And perhaps we could go in Joe's truck and show her the land?'

'One look at that patch o' scrub and she'll wipe yer,' said Pat.

'No, Pat. She knows all about it.'

'About livin' in a tent?'

'Yes.'

'Gees, she must have ut bad, too.'

I shaved my face again, and put on my best suit to visit Kay's parents. Pat and Dennis wished me luck very solemnly, and asked me what kind of flowers I want on my grave. I wondered whether it was the custom in Australia to take flowers on such occasions. They answered me it was. They were going to town, and accompanied me on the train. I bought the flowers at Central. They gave me careful instructions about carrying them, and said that immediately I met Kay's mother, I was to bow deeply and say, 'Beautiful flowers for a beautiful lady.' Then I was to kiss her hand, hit her over the head with the flowers and say, 'To hell with all mothers-in-law. Workers of the world, unite.' I promised I would do this, and got on a tram for the Quay. When I looked back, they were standing together, looking very serious. Dennis called out, 'Good luck mate.' I felt sad, as though I were leaving them forever. This was foolish. When I saw the people on the tram smiling at me, I felt foolish also.

When I met Kay at Manly, she said, 'Flowers, Nino?'

'For your mother,' I told her.

'Sweet,' she said. 'She'll love them.'

'Should I take a gift to your father also?'

'Of course not. Is that your best suit?'

'Yes.'

'Dad's all done up in his too.' She took my arm.

'Have you told him?'

'Yes.'

'And have you told him about the tent?'

'No. I'll leave that to you. But I told him we were getting married in September. Is that all right with you? I'd like to be married in the spring.'

'That is very much all right with me.'

'Good.' She pressed my arm. 'Gee, Nino, I can't believe it.'

When we reached her home, I began to feel a little nervous. Her mother came to the door.

Kay said, 'Here he is,' and introduced us.

I said, 'How do you do?' and gave her the flowers.

She said, 'For me? They're lovely. Come inside. Dad's waiting in the lounge like a cat on hot bricks. He's already smoked four pipes since lunch. You said he was big, Kay, but not that big. Dad will get a surprise.'

We had reached the lounge. She opened the door; Kay's father was sitting by the fire. He got up. He was big, also. She said, 'Dad, here's Nino. He brought me some flowers. Aren't they lovely?'

He grunted and held out his hand.

'Glad to know yer,' he said. 'Sit down.'

I took his hand and said, 'How do you do, sir?'

He turned his chair away from the fire and sat down. Kay sat on the sofa, and her mother took the chair on the other side of the fire. I sat beside Kay. Both her parents looked at me, her mother with a polite smile, and her father as though I were applying for a job. I looked at Kay. She seemed confident, and pressed my hand. The silence became embarrassing. I began to get irritable with her father. Finally he said, 'Heard a lot about you.'

I said, 'I have had heard a lot about you, too. You are a builder, and you think writers are parasites, and you do not like bricklayers, and you can't stand Italians. I am a writer and a bricklayer and an Italian. I am going to marry your daughter.'

'Wow,' said Kay. 'That's telling him.'

Her mother looked worried, she stood up. She said, 'I'll just put these flowers in some water, and make a cup of tea.'

'I'll help you,' Kay said. She pressed my hand again, and went out with her mother.

'Close the door,' her father said.

She put the tip of her tongue towards him, smiled at me, and closed the door. I could hear their voices fading as they went towards the kitchen. Then there was silence again.

'Pretty sure of yourself aren't yer?' her father said.

'Yes.'

'Kay seems ter think a lot of yer.'

'I think a lot of Kay.'

'Hurt her in any way an' I'll break yer neck, d'yer understand that?'

'If I hurt her in any way, I'll break my own neck, d'yer understand that?'

'Hm. Wot sorta writin' der yer do?'

'I wrote for Italian magazines. Now I lay bricks.'

'Mug's game.'

'I do not agree.'

'Reckon my daughter c'n do better than marry a brickie.'

'She has chosen to marry a brickie.'

'September she tells me.'

'Yes.'

'Got a house?'

'I have the land. I will build a house.'

'Not by September, yer won't.'

'We will live in a tent until it is built.'

'In a tent? Wotta yer plannin' ter do? Dump my daughter down on a bit o' land an' build a home around 'er?'

'Yes.'

'Not if I c'n stop yer.'

'You can't.'

'H'm. Dago ain't yer?'

'No. I am Italian.'

'Dago. Yer bigger than most of 'em, but yer still a Dago.'

'You should be pleased.'

'Pleased? Why?'

'You have a picture of one on your wall. In the place of honour.'

'The Pope?'

'Yes. Eugenio Pacelli. We are both Italians. If I am a Dago so is he. So also are most of the College of Cardinals.'

'H'm. Reckon we'll ever have an Australian Pope?'

'It is possible. If Kay has a son, perhaps he will be the first.'

'Cripes. Don't think much of yerself do yer. Born in a tent?'

'The Founder of the Church was born in a stable.'

'H'm. Gunna be a brickie all yer life?'

'Perhaps. I do not know. Australia is a good country. A man can be whatever he likes here.'

'Yer right about that. Reckon yer might take on buildin'?'

'It is possible.'

'Ut's a hard game. I c'n give you a few hints might save yer a lot o' headaches.'

'I will remember that. Thank you, sir.'

'No need ter call me sir, son.' He got up. 'How about a drop o' whisky? Sorta celebrate the occasion, eh?'

'I could do with a drop of whisky,' I said.

'So could I, be cripes. Gettin' acquainted takes ut out o' yer.' He was at the sideboard. 'Take yer coat an' tie orf. Ut's warm enough in here. How do yer like ut?'

'With water, thanks.'

'So do I.'

We removed our coats and ties. When Kay and her mother returned we were drinking whisky and discussing building. They carried trays with scones, cakes, sandwiches and tea.

Her mother said, 'Well. Look at that.'

Kay said, 'Told you it wouldn't take them long.'

They removed the whisky and set the tea things down.

Kay's father said, 'First bloke that's stood up ter me fer years.'

'About time, too,' said her mother.

'Yer gettin' a man here,' he told Kay. 'Reckon he's gunna be the boss.'

'I hope so,' she said.

Chapter Thirteen

I took her out to Punchbowl. Jimmy and his wife Betty were there. Pat and Dennis were there. They wore their suits, with collars and ties. They were all very polite, and Edie served afternoon tea. With cake forks. When they weren't looking at Kay and saying nothing, they talked about the weather. I had told Kay about my friends, and she said she was looking forward to meeting them. She said they sounded fun. They weren't fun. They behaved as though they were at a funeral. Joe said it was colder than usual for this time of the year. The others agreed. Pat said it would probably be colder next month. Dennis said there was a very heavy frost yesterday morning. Yes, they had noticed that. August was the worst month, with those winds. Yes, it was. They were getting on well with the new school. Yes, they were. Campbell and Smith had a good team. Yes, they had. Building was a cold job, this weather. Yes, it was. Kay was saying nothing, but once she winked at me. I began to get irritable. Edie said, brightly, 'Nino and Kay are getting married in September.' Betty said that would be nice. Joe asked each of us in turn if we would like some more tea. Edie asked each of us to eat some more cake.

I said, in a loud voice, 'Bring out the bloody beer.' This was followed by complete silence. They all turned their heads quickly, and looked at Kay. They became quite still.

Even Jimmy's brown fingers, holding a half rolled cigarette, became motionless.

Kay said calmly, 'Bloody good idea.'

'Whacko,' yelled Pat, and rushed out the back door, closely followed by Dennis. They went over the back fence. Joe went out the front door, and around to the side of the house, closely followed by Jimmy. Edie and Betty disappeared into the front room.

Kay put her hand on my knee. 'Thank you, Nino. Poor dears. They were trying so hard.' She smiled at me.

I said, 'I was getting mad at them.'

'They were only waiting for a signal to relax. It was a beautiful signal.'

We both began to laugh.

Edie called out, 'What's so funny? Kay, come in here a minute.'

Kay went in. I went to my room and changed into an old pair of trousers and sweater. Joe and Jimmy returned carrying bottles of beer. They put them down. They looked at me. Without saying anything, they went out to the garage, and came back wearing their old winter working clothes. Joe said, ' 'Owyergoing Nino—orright?'

I said, 'Orright mate.'

'She's easy on the eyes,' he said.

Jimmy agreed, 'Not 'ard ter take at all.'

Dennis yelled from the back, 'Hey Nino . . . give us a hand.'

I went out and he and Pat passed more beer over the fence. 'Got 'is drinkin' togs on,' Pat said.

'Bloody gettin' ours on, too,' said Dennis. 'Be with yer in a minute, Nino.'

They went into their house. I carried the beer into Joe's place. He and Jimmy were busy filling glasses.

'Stack 'em in the kitchen matey,' Joe said. 'The sheilas will be out in a minute.'

I did so, and returned to the lounge. Joe said, 'Wait fer Dennis an' Pat.'

We did not have to wait long. They also had changed into old clothes. Dennis wore his old straw hat, upside down. He carried his mouth organ, and put it on the mantelpiece. Joe presented each of us with a full glass.

'Sorry about the bloody afternoon tea,' he said. 'Edie's idea.'

'Gotta give 'em their 'eads,' Pat said. 'Nino's idea's better.'

'Here's ter the bride,' said Joe.

We drank to the bride. Joe refilled the glasses.

Pat said, 'Wot I can't get over is 'im findin' 'er without any help from us.'

Dennis objected, 'Wodda yer mean no help from us? We told 'im where ter look, didn' we?'

'Didn' reckon 'e'd do any good, but. Didn' even reckon 'e was fair dinkum.'

'Slashin' line.'

'Yeah. We shoulda gone with 'im.'

'We're doin' orright.'

'Not right now, we ain't.'

'Soon fix that. Use yer phone, Joe?'

'Go ahead matey.'

Dennis went to the phone. The girls came in.

Joe said, 'Wodda youse been up to?'

'Fixing our faces,' Edie said.

'Didn' make 'em look any better. Have a beer.'

They accepted. Pat led Kay to the centre of the room, and walked slowly around her, inspecting her carefully.

'Not real bad,' he said. 'Think I'll 'ave a go at takin' 'er orf yer, Nino.'

'Nino might object,' Kay said.

' 'Im? Couldn' fight 'is way out of a paper bag.'

Dennis came in. 'All fixed. Be here in 'alf an hour.'

'Who?' said Edie.

'Coupla dames.'

'More the merrier,' Joe said.

Dennis said to Pat, 'Wodda you doin' there with Kay? That's my possie. Have a beer, Kay.'

'I have one, thanks.'

'Well, yer got two hands. Have another one.' She laughed and accepted it. 'That's wot I like ter see. A dame with a beer in each hand. Now tell us the story of yer life.'

'I was born. I went to school. I left school. I went to work. I met Nino.'

'That all?'

'That's all so far.'

'Far enough too. Can yer cook?'

'Yes.'

'Can yer sew?'

'Yes.'

'Do you know yer gunna live in a tent?'

'Yes.'

'There'll be flies an' ants an' fleas an' beetles an' spiders an' scorpions an' lizards.'

'Don't forget the possums,' Pat said.

'Yeah, an' possums. They'll pinch yer bread an' sugar an' pull yer hair.'

'I love possums.'

'There y'are Nino. Two timin' yer already. She loves possums.'

'Not the right girl fer you at all, mate. More my type.'

'Your type? Only find your type in the Zoo.'

Kay said, 'Don't you like faithful women, Pat?'

'Dunno. Never seen one.'

'You're seeing one now.'

'Take yer word for ut. Mean ter say yer gunna stick to old Nino?'

'For the rest of my life, if he'll put up with me.'

'Not much fun fer us in that.'

Dennis said, 'Reckon we're wastin' our time, Pat?'

'Looks like ut.'

'Reckon we better stick ter beer?'

'Until them other two skirts turn up.'

'Yeah.' He held Kay's arm in his hand. 'Take her other arm.'

Pat did so. They led her over to me.

'Nino, we'd like yer ter meet Kay.'

'How do you do, Kay.'

'How do you do, Nino.'

'She's all yours mate.'

'Thank you gentlemen.'

'Don't thank us. Ut was her idea. Never met a woman with any sense yet.'

'Wot's 'e got that we haven't got?'

'Kay.'

'Yeah. Know wot'll happen, Kay, if you don't play straight with Nino?'

'He'll bump me on the head.'

'Yeah, he would too. But after that . . . after that, mind yer . . . we'll chuck you into a concrete mixer.'

'Oo lovely,' Kay said. 'They go round and round.'

Dennis made circles at the side of his head, with his finger. 'Bats,' he said.

'Nutty as a fruit cake,' said Pat.

'We're sorry for yer, Nino, old boy. Yer've drawn a ning nong.'

'Loves possums.'

'An' concrete mixers.'

'Gone in the scone.'

'Nothing there, man. Absolutely nothing there.'

'Very sad, poor Nino.'

Kay said, 'May I have my arms now? I want to drink my beer.'

'Whacko!' said Dennis. 'Ut was only temporary. She's sane again.'

'Sane as you an' me.'

'Now yer got me worried.'

The visit was a success. They liked Kay. Kay liked them. She still does. The party was still going when we left to go back to Manly. It was still going when I returned at one o'clock in the morning. And Kay didn't see our land until the next week-end.

Each week-end until we were married, we worked on it. Sometimes she and I worked alone, but more often our friends helped us. We met our neighbours, who were very friendly, and gave us tea and advice. Australians like giving people tea and advice. The tea is always very good, and sometimes the advice too. But it is difficult to know when an Australian is giving you serious advice or pulling your leg. This latter term is used to describe foolish advice given in a serious manner. All Australians are very fond of this pastime, and our neighbours were not exceptions. But Kay was usually able to detect it. We cleared the land, fenced it, and built a fibro store shed. Joe drew the plan of the house for me, and submitted it to the local council, who raised no objection. And I bought the tent. I also bought a second-hand utility truck. This did not leave much money in the bank.

We were married at Manly in September. My father sent his blessing, and my mother wrote to say that the picture of

Kay reminded her of that little Maria who went away from our village to marry that awful shopkeeper in Firenze with the big ears and the gold teeth. They had five children, now, and she looked terrible last time she was home. My father said that Italy was going to the dogs. There were three Meridionali in the village now, and they refused to go away, even in the winter. And Signor Cuccu had joined the Communista. My father had beaten him with his stick, and members of the Communista had broken three of my father's windows, and poisoned the black cat. He was still mayor, but the Polizia were no good, and he suspected them of Communist sympathies. My mother said her rheumatism had been much better lately, but my father was becoming difficult in his old age. He had had a terrible fight with that nice Signor Cuccu, because Signor Cuccu had been seen talking to a Communist from Milano who was visiting our old church. The house was in need of repairs, but father was too mean to have it done. Three of the windows had been broken in a storm, and were still broken. And the cat had died of old age and was buried under the oleander tree near the lavatory. My father said I should stay in Australia, where the only enemies were snakes and kangaroos and savages. He supposed my intended wife was an English girl, and she must be very brave. But the English were always being very brave, and going off to strange places. I was very brave, too, and he was proud of me, because I had lived up to my name. I must be very careful not to allow any of my children to be eaten by kangaroos, and the first boy must be named Giovanni. If I was short of weapons I must write and tell him, because Signor Guareschi's double barrelled shotgun was for sale, and he could get it cheap because Signor Guareschi had bought a Vespa, and was in debt.

I translated the letters for Kay, and she asked me hadn't I told my parents what life in Sydney was really like? I said I had, but they probably thought I was exaggerating, so as not to cause them worry. But she said surely they had read my articles in the magazines? This was undoubtedly true, but my father probably considered that the Press was controlled by the Communista, and these articles had not been written by me at all, but were propaganda to entice all the brave Italians to go to Australia so that the Communista could take over the country without having to fight. Kay thought that this was most unlikely, but I have since learned from my mother that I was right.

Our wedding was like Jimmy and Betty's wedding, which I have already described, except that this time I was the bunny, instead of being just a guest. I expected to be very proud of Kay, and very tender towards her, and to make a good speech and say these things gracefully. But when the time came, my mind seemed to have received an anaesthetic, and refused to function. This anaesthetic also affected my memory, because very few of the details are clear to me now. I can remember only Kay's eyelashes resting on her cheeks as we knelt at the altar, and a small shaving cut on the priest's chin, and somebody sneezing behind us. Then there is a picture of photographers' flash bulbs, and too many people in Kay's parents' house, and myself standing up and speaking in Italian. I do not remember what I said, but Kay says everyone was very surprised, and that just before I sat down, I said in English. 'There's Joe. He hates weddings. Howyergoin'mateorright?'

I remember wondering what happened to Kay's white dress, because I suddenly saw her coming towards me in a grey one. I remember her mother crying and myself telling her that my mother was probably crying too, because she was very fond of the cat. I remember her father's wide grin as he slapped me on the back and gave me a whisky. I do not remember drinking the whisky, but I do remember wondering why we were crossing the harbour bridge in a car, instead of being down there on the blue water in a ferry. We were in an aeroplane when my mind cleared and I really saw Kay for the first time that day. Then I was proud and felt very tender towards her, but it was a bit late. However, she didn't seem to mind, and told me that it had been a lovely wedding, and that I was quite mad. This I knew. She said we must not appear to be a honeymoon couple, so I looked out the window with interest at a part of Australia I had not previously seen. And the hostess brought us a parcel containing chocolates and cigarettes and a card which read: 'To the newlyweds from the Captain and Crew'. Kay said that she supposed it was no use trying to hide the fact that we were just married, so we might as well enjoy it.

We spent two weeks in a rented cottage at Coff's Harbour, and I finally learned to crack a wave, and was very proud of myself. Then we returned to our tent, and my bricklaying, and our week-end building. The neighbours had put flowers in the tent, and food in the ice chest, and came over to wish us 'welcome home'. Kay cried a little because she said they were so kind. They are still so kind, and I am glad that I have been able to repay their kindness a little by helping them with their building problems. Because now I am no longer a bricklayer, but a true builder in partnership with Kay's father. I look after the work on this side of the harbour, and he looks after the north side. He has taught me much, and I am very grateful to him. We are good friends.

Now it is Sunday morning again, and the summer is nearly finished. So is this story, my first in English. It has been written mostly at week-ends, since I finished building my home. And to-day the sun is shining again after weeks of much rain, as it was shining when I started to write early in the summer. I have just returned from our little church, and Kay is up there now, and I am supposed to be minding young Nino. He is inside the house somewhere. He toddles around and gets into much mischief, and falls over often, but if anything happens he will yell, and I know. He is good at yelling. We hope his sister Maria will be with us in June. I wanted her named Kay, but my wife says if she is a girl she is to be named Maria. So she will be named Maria.

It seems to me that in this story I have frequently deserted my subject, which was to have been the Australian language. But writing is like that. All kinds of thoughts come into your head, and find themselves on paper. For example, now I find myself thinking of young Nino, and how fortunate he is to have been born in this country. Probably he will never learn to speak Italian. Probably I will forget it myself, and will have difficulty conversing with my parents when we go to visit them. But there is one thing I know. I do not think that in this country he will ever be hungry. I have read and heard men speak of the time known as the 'Depression', when I was only a small boy in Italy. But I have not read or heard of any Australian actually dying of hunger. This cannot be said of Europe. It is a terrible thing to see people dying of hunger. I cannot imagine what must be the feelings of a parent to see his child dying of hunger. I think hunger is the most powerful motive force that can affect humans. In spite of my religion, I am not at all sure that I would not steal and kill if my children were starving. It is good to know that there is at least one country in the world where he who works will eat. And there is room for so many more people to come here to work and eat. I put the map of Italy on the map of Australia, and I think of the millions of people who live in little Italy, and I do not know how many millions could live in Australia. But it is very many millions. I am very fortunate that five years ago my boss sent me here, and if God is good, here I will remain.

I have been told by Australians who have what is known as 'itchy feet', that a man who decides to build a house on a piece of land and live there for the remainder of his life, is no better than a cabbage. But this is not true. A cabbage has no alternative, and I have. A cabbage is imprisoned in its plot of ground by the man who owns it, but I am free to leave mine, if I wish. That is the only true freedom. The freedom to go away, it is something that so many people in Europe and Asia do not have. If I were forced to remain here, and forbidden to go to Queensland, I would probably be violent in my efforts to go there. But because I am free to go there, I have never been, and am content to remain here. Human beings are very perverse. Shackle them and you have trouble. Leave them free, and they will shackle themselves. I can imagine the violent reactions from a pair of these Australian itchy feet if they were forbidden to return home. Anyone who tried to put fetters on the feet of Joe, Dennis or Pat would have real trouble. And these are not unusual men. They are typical. We have them in this suburb, too. Here I know Aub and Tony, Bob and Jacko, Addo, Simmo, Peto and Old Vic, and I would not like to be the man who tried to restrict their physical freedom. Nor would I like to try to bump on the head little Bertie with the big piano accordion, or Big Jim with the tiny ukulele. These were here at our home last Friday night. We did not invite them, but they were here.

They were here because in New South Wales now the hotels do not close until ten o'clock. This does not make sense, but it's true. We have a hotel in our suburb. There is only one, but it is a very nice little hotel. The proprietor's name is Micky. This always amuses me, because a man named Micky should be a little man with bright eyes like Bertie, and this Micky is a big man who is very expert at chucking people out if they become obnoxious. Of course, the only people who become obnoxious are visitors. None of our people ever become obnoxious. This is probably because they know how good Micky is at chucking out. Our hotel does not become crowded with too many people, as some hotels do, and it is very pleasant after a hot day's work. Sometimes one of our neighbours offers to mind young Nino so that Kay and I can go out. Usually this is when some picture show is on, which we wish to see. But sometimes we are told that we are staying home too much, and we are ordered to go out. One of our neighbours is an elderly lady who gives orders very firmly and objecting to them is useless. So last Friday evening, which was very hot, we received an order, and went out.

We did not wish to see the picture show, and it was too hot to go into the City to see one there, so Kay asked me to take her to the local pub 'for a couple of quiet beers'. She is well known there, because she often goes in for a quiet beer after she has done her shopping. She and Micky are good friends. So we went in for these quiet beers, and sat at one of the little tables amongst the cool ferns and flowers. And Aub and Tony came in and joined us, and we talked and sipped our beer, and it was very pleasant. Bob and his wife appeared, and Jacko and his wife, and other small tables were brought up to ours, and Bertie and Big Jim arrived. They all said they came out because it was too hot to stay home. So we had music, and quiet songs, and everybody else in the hotel joined with us. Until we heard

Micky's voice announcing that bed and breakfast cost nineteen and six, and we knew it was nearly ten o'clock. And Aub suggested that we go up to the club, and I thought Kay would be too tired, but she said she wasn't.

So we went up to the club, 'just for a little while', and Addo and Peto and Simmo and Old Vic were there. It was getting late, and Kay and I said we had to go, because our neighbour was 'minding the monster' and she would be wanting to go to bed. And Addo said that in that case they would all come down to my place, and I could make coffee. So about twenty people got into cars and came to our place, and I made coffee for all, and Bertie and Big Jim played music, and the elderly lady was so excited she stayed and had coffee also. And Peto paid her a lot of attention with exaggerated gallantry, and gave her whisky and beer, of which there was plenty because everybody had brought something from the club. There were not enough chairs, but most of these were unoccupied anyway, as they seemed to prefer to sit on the floor. There were not enough coffee cups either, but they drank from glasses.

The men washed up, and only broke two glasses and no cups. Whilst the elderly lady was singing a song, 'Goodbye Dolly' I think, Kay was having a very intense discussion on politics with Addo and Old Vic, Aub and Tony and I were getting animated over the question of racial intolerance, and Peto and Simmo and Jacko were heatedly helping the women to reorganise the education system. Bertie's wide grin somehow managed to keep his cigarette holder in place, and Big Jim solemnly strummed his minute ukulele. I realised that it was one o'clock in the morning, and we were having a do. I thought Kay should be in bed, and told her so, and she patted me on the head and said, 'Thank you darling,' and went on talking. And it seemed only a few minutes later that Bob entered from the kitchen carrying great stacks of buttered toast, and saying, 'Breakfast everybody. The sun's up.'

It was too. The elderly lady said, 'My goodness! I haven't stayed up all night since nineteen eighteen.' She was still excited, and very proud of herself, and went away to feed her fowls, happily singing a song called 'Daisy'. Kay wanted to know where Bob had got the bread for all that toast, as she knew we didn't have that much. He wouldn't say. His wife wanted to know where he'd been all night, as she hadn't seen him since about one o'clock, but again he wouldn't say. Bob is a big cheerful man who can give no information with much charm.

The toast was all eaten and young Nino came in with much energy, and belligerently demanded his breakfast. He also surveyed our visitors sternly and said, 'My place. Go home.' So they went home, and we fed young Nino, and Kay went to bed.

I am convinced that I am unable to sleep in the daytime, so I sat down to write some more of this story, and immediately went to sleep. I was awakened at three o'clock in the afternoon by Bob. He offered me a cold beer.

'Hair of the dog,' he said. 'Do yer good.'

I said, 'How long have you been here?'

'Just brought the young bloke back. Took him down this morning to play with the kids. He's had 'is lunch. Feel like comin' down to the pub?'

I said, 'No. I never want to see that place again.'

He laughed. 'Cleaned up the house for yer. How does she look?'

'She' looked clean and tidy, and I said so, and thanked him.

'Nothin' to ut. How's the book goin'? Am I in ut?'

I said it was going well but he was not in it.

I said, 'Would you like to be in it?'

'Yeah. Bung me in.'

So there you are Bob, you are in. And in your own phrase, 'It couldn't happen to a nicer bloke.'

That episode of Friday night and yesterday illustrates the informality of the Australian way of life, and the Australian's unquenchable energy and thirst. He works hard, with much cursing and swearing, and is most unhappy when he has no work to do. He loves beer and tobacco, and impassioned arguments. He is kind and generous and abusive. He will swear at you, and call you insulting names, and love you like a brother. He is without malice. He will fight you with skill and ferocity, and buy you a beer immediately afterwards. He is a man of many contradictions, but his confidence and self-sufficing are inspiring. If he is beaten in a fight or an argument, he laughs about it the next day, and tells his mates, 'The bastard was too good fer me.' He doesn't resent a defeat, but is queerly proud of the physical or mental ability of 'that bastard who done me over'. It takes a European a long time to begin to understand him.

I once heard a Sydney Australian describe the citizens of Melbourne as being 'a weird mob'. His listeners appeared to be completely satisfied with the description, and to understand immediately all that it implied. At that time I did not understand it at all. Now I think I do. It seems to mean that it is very difficult for a citizen of Sydney to understand the citizens of Melbourne, who appear to be interested in such extraordinary things as Australian Rules football, calm water for swimming, and six o'clock closing. Yet they brew magnificent beer, and like to eat Sydney oysters. Their policemen wear strange uniforms, and their electric trains are queer. I have not seen Melbourne, but have been told these things. They are very disparaging about Sydney's beautiful harbour, and very proud of a muddy creek called the Yarra. They would probably be decent blokes when you got to know them, but it would take years. Their ways are not our ways, therefore they are a weird mob. Certainly from the point of view of a European migrant, the citizens of Sydney are a weird mob. It takes years to understand them, but the understanding, when it comes, is infinitely rewarding. It is not possible to understand them at all until you have learned their queer, abbreviated language. Joe asked me the other day what I was 'gunna do with the young bloke when 'e grows up'. I said I did not know, and Joe said, 'Cut 's fingers orf before yer make a brickie out of 'im.' This appears to mean that I should first cut off young Nino's fingers, and then instruct him in the art of laying bricks. What Joe meant was that cutting off his fingers was the lesser of two evils, and that, if faced with the alternative, I should do this, rather than let him learn to lay bricks. Any Australian would understand immediately all the shades of meaning in such use of the word 'before'. No New Australian would. The better his knowledge of English, the more puzzled he would be.

And when Kay says, 'I thought you were supposed to be minding young Nino,' and I agree, and she says, 'He's only down in the shed with your tins of paint,' I learn how an Australian can use that little word 'only' to convey complex meanings, otherwise needing whole sentences. It gives me a picture of young Nino surrounded by tins of paint with the lids off, with paint all over the floor of the shed and all over himself, and his hair which was brushed and combed this morning, and probably in his mouth also, which will make him sick and we will have to send for the doctor. All this, that one little word tells me, and it also severely rebukes me for neglecting my duty. None of these meanings will be found in a dictionary.

I praise the dinner that Kay has cooked, and tell her it is the best dinner that I have had for years, and she says, 'It wasn't that good,' and the little word 'that' tells me more than you would think any word could.

Australians are incredibly economical with words, and also with diction and gestures. They open their mouths no more than is absolutely necessary, and rely on emphasis more than on explanatory gestures. Whereas an Italian does not mind what sort of faces he is pulling as long as the sounds he is making are clear, and uses his arms and hands and shoulders to make them clearer still, an Australian will devastate you with a few short words delivered with an expressionless face, and from almost closed lips. These words will not be clearly pronounced, will be given an accent and inflexion unintelligible to a student of English, and will not mean what they appear to mean. So that you will not be devastated until you have learned the language, and then you will be able to devastate him with an appropriate reply delivered the same way, and you will be friends. Until then, you will just be a 'bloody New Australian', and regarded as something of a nuisance because things have to be explained to you all the time. And because you don't understand the explanation either, you will be regarded as a dill, and left alone in your loneliness. Mix with Australians, listen to them, work with them, and practise in secret the sentences you hear, so that you can say them exactly as you heard them. Do much more listening than talking because they will resent having to cease using their own verbal short-hand to explain things to you. When you are working with them, they will ridicule you in hundreds of ways, but never lose your temper because this ridicule is natural to them, and is not hostile. If you lose your temper you will have declared war, and you will certainly lose the war also. By keeping your temper you will win their respect; by learning their language you will win their liking. And when somebody says to you, 'Yer know wot yer c'n do yer bastard,' and you say, 'Yeah, an' you know wot you c'n do,' and he says to the barmaid, 'Give us another one fer this drongo' you know that you have been accepted, and will soon be an Australian and your troubles will be over.

But if you are ever told that you are a 'bludger', go home. A bludger is the worst thing you can be in Australia. It means that you are criminally lazy, that you 'pole on yer mates', that you are a 'piker'—a mean, contemptible, miserable individual who is not fit to associate with human beings. No one will talk to you, or buy you a drink, and you've had it. You will be called a bastard because you are a good bloke, but if you are called a bludger you probably are one. You might be called a 'bludgin' bastard' in a rueful sort of way which is half admiring but the word bludger by itself is final condemnation.

So watch it, Charlie. Return all shouts, pull your weight on the job, if you have cigarettes offer them to others; if a man does you a favour, return it sometime. But don't overdo the generosity. That will make you a 'crawler' which is nearly as bad as being a bludger. And don't abuse anybody until you have made friends. You may abuse friends as much as you like. You will be expected to. But only in public. With others present, your abuse of your friend is a public declaration of friendship, which is much appreciated. Abuse him in private, when there is no one else present, and you've got trouble. You will have lost your friend. Unless you have a fight, and blood is shed. Everything will be all right then.

There are far too many New Australians in this country who are still mentally living in their homelands, who mix with people of their own nationality, and try to retain their own language and customs. Who even try to persuade Australians to adopt their customs and manners. Cut it out. There is no better way of life in the world than that of the Australian. I firmly believe this. The grumbling, growling, cursing, profane, laughing, beer drinking, abusive, loyal-to-his-mates Australian is one of the few free men left on this earth. He fears no one, crawls to no one, bludges on no one, and acknowledges no master. Learn his way. Learn his language. Get yourself accepted as one of him; and you will enter a world that you never dreamed existed. And once you have entered it, you will never leave it.

Recently, in the street, I heard a mother chastising her child in voluble Italian. And this small boy said to his mother, 'Gees mum, I dunno wot yer talkin' about.' I was very pleased. I told Kay. She said, 'It must be hard for the parents.' Of course it's hard. But the kids can do it. They do it by mixing with Australian kids, and listening. The adults can do it by mixing with Australian adults. All that is needed is the will to learn. Well, don't be bludgers. Hop in and learn. I've heard parents in shops talking to kids in their homeland language, and the kids translating into English, and making the purchases. This is disgraceful. Those parents should be bloody ashamed of themselves. They came to this country because their own is impossible and by their own laziness make this one impossible for themselves also. It makes me very irritable.

If I keep on thinking about this I will be irritable at dinner, which smells good, and then Kay will say I am in one of my 'dirty Italian moods' again. So I will not think about it any more. I will stop writing now, and count my blessings. They are very numerous. I will stop worrying about these New Australians, and start wondering what I am going to do this afternoon. There are so many things I can do. I can work in my garden, or fix the electric iron which I should have fixed last week and which Kay will need to-morrow. Or I can take her and young Nino into the Domain, and listen to the ratbags making speeches. Or we can all go down to Cronulla for a swim. Or we can visit Bob, and eat some of his oysters. Or go and talk to Joe about building, while Kay and Edie gossip as women do. There are hundreds of ways we could spend this sunny Sunday afternoon. Or we could just stay at home and do nothing, and perhaps that would be best of all. To rest on the seventh day. To thank God for letting us be here. To thank Him for letting me be an Australian. Sometimes I think that if I am ever fortunate enough to reach Heaven, I will know I am there when I hear Him say, 'Howyergoin'mate orright?'